TABOR EVANS

LONGARM

AND THE DIAMOND SNATCHERS

NOV -- 2013

JOVE BOOKS, NEW YORK

LONGARM AND THE DIAMOND SNATCHERS

A Jove Book / published by arrangement with
the author

PRINTING HISTORY
Jove edition / May 1993

All rights reserved.
Copyright © 1993 by Jove Publications, Inc.
Rails West! excerpt copyright © 1993 by Jove Publications, Inc.
This book may not be reproduced in whole or in part,
by mimeograph or any other means, without permission.
For information address: The Berkley Publishing Group,
200 Madison Avenue, New York, NY 10016.

ISBN: 0-515-11103-1

Jove Books are published by The Berkley Publishing Group,
200 Madison Avenue, New York, New York 10016.
The name "JOVE" and the "J" logo
are trademarks belonging to Jove Publications, Inc.

PRINTED IN THE UNITED STATES OF AMERICA

10 9 8 7 6 5 4 3 2 1

Chapter 1

A rifle round powdered dust from a granite outcropping just to Custis Long's left and screamed off into the Colorado high country like an outraged parlor girl. Long bellied down a little deeper in the snowbank and chanced a look around the base of a big Englemann spruce.

Two bank robbers hid in the trees ahead. Only two left of four who'd cleaned out the Loveland First State Bank three days ago and taken off into the Rocky Mountains on snowshoes, hoping no one would track them.

United States Deputy Marshal Custis Long had arrived by train in Loveland yesterday. The chase led him here after the first bank heist by the Galloway gang a week ago. Now he had the last two outlaws cowering in this small valley that backed up against a mountain, with two huge snowfields overhead. No way out that direction.

The robbers and killers had no place to run. The small cabin they'd come here to find lay flattened under tons of snow from an earlier avalanche. Now the two outlaws hunkered down behind big Douglas fir and blue spruce trees with a shootout their only option.

Flint Galloway, leader of the Galloway gang, would never give up. In prison he'd told anyone who would listen that he'd never go back to jail. He'd rather die first.

1

United States Deputy Marshal Custis Long, known around the West as Longarm, rested his Colt Lightning carbine on the snow and checked the big fir where he'd last seen Galloway. He spotted an errant brown boot showing around the side of the tree.

Longarm refined his sight down the rifle, looked away a moment, came back, and zeroed in on the half a boot. He fired. A scream of protest and pain echoed through the Colorado Rockies. Six return-fire rounds blasted harmlessly into the tree protecting Longarm.

The combatants huddled in the snow only forty yards apart, shooting-gallery range for their rifles. The man who made the first mistake would die.

Longarm checked around the other side of the three-foot-thick Englemann and saw movement. Galloway's one remaining gang member darted to another tree. He moved away from Galloway, maybe to get Longarm in a cross fire, the marshal decided. Longarm guessed the robber's next move. He'd try for the big fir twenty feet farther to the left.

Longarm moved his rifle sights halfway between the two trees and waited.

Two minutes later a green coat blur showed by one tree as the robber sprinted fifteen feet toward his next cover. Longarm had guessed correctly. He sighted on the runner, tracked him a second, led him by a foot, and fired. The Colt carbine's big .44–40 slug jolted into the outlaw's chest, cut a wide swath through his heart, and dumped him lifeless in the snow five feet from his protection.

"Bastard!" Galloway shouted from behind his tree.

"Toss out your rifle and live another month or two," Longarm bellowed. Two rifle rounds slammed into the marshal's Englemann spruce as a response.

A stand off. Both men armed, both good shots, so close neither could miss. Longarm looked for some advantage. Galloway had his back to the cliff, nowhere he could run. Longarm had seen the outlaw's shoulder bag full of ammunition, and his two rifles. He could hold out until dark and then vanish over the white snow and get away clean.

Longarm looked at the cliff again. Yes, he should have thought of it before. The plan should work. He scanned the hillside, and the bulging twenty-foot-thick blanket of snow resting there, until he found the right spot. The deputy U.S. marshal lifted his carbine and aimed.

He fired four times, as quickly as he could lever in new rounds, his target a stunted blue spruce halfway up the one-hundred-foot cliff behind Galloway. The last two shots had the effect he wanted. The spruce sagged sideways, top-heavy with two-day-old snow. The marshal's rifle rounds found the vital inch-thick top of the tree where it bowed with the snow's weight. The rounds snapped off the top three feet of the spruce and its two hundred pounds of snow. The weight dropped suddenly onto the teetering bank of heavy snowpack below.

The new snow started a small slide. It grew and built, and then the entire section of the snow, fifty-feet wide, shook loose and cascaded down the last seventy-five feet of cliff to the drop-off.

Flint Galloway must have heard the snow coming. Longarm knew Galloway had only two choices—to stay where he was or to try to outrun the avalanche as it thundered toward him. Galloway ran.

Longarm spotted him, tracked the killer in his brown overcoat until he was out of the direct path of the avalanche, then fired his rifle twice. His second round caught Galloway in the left thigh and slammed him into the snow beside an old-growth Douglas fir.

Longarm put another round into the snow in front of Galloway as a warning. The snow mass smashed into the trees and brush well behind the outlaw. The rumbling sound of the crashing snow stopped, leaving the cold winter scene whisper silent.

"Move again and you're frozen buzzard lunch," Longarm brayed. "Hands in the air. Sit up and don't touch that rifle or your six-gun."

Longarm figured the man would roll behind the tree and keep shooting. Instead he dropped the rifle he still carried and held his hands high. It took Longarm a minute and a half to charge through the snow to where the killer sat, hands still grabbing at the sky.

Three days later, Galloway sat in jail in Loveland and Longarm had taken the train back to Denver. His report lay on Chief U.S. Marshal Billy Vail's desk. Longarm had attended a traveling

3

stage play the night before with a pretty blond lady he knew. Now he wanted to get back to work.

He paused in the outer office of the First District Court of Colorado and scowled at Henry, Billy's prissy clerk, who excelled in efficiency.

"The marshal is busy at the moment, Deputy Long. He said you should wait a minute or two. There's a new copy of the *Police Gazette* over there for your enjoyment."

Soft frown wrinkles creased Longarm's forehead. He was a lean, lantern-jawed man, with a mustache that swept wide and curled upward at each end. He had raw-boned features, and skin burned leather-brown from the wind, snow, and sun.

"Why you being so everlasting polite this morning, Henry?" Longarm asked.

Henry shrugged. "Maybe it's because I know the tough job you have coming up." He held up both hands in a quick protest. "Maybe it's because of nothing."

Longarm's blue-gray eyes studied the clerk but could find nothing out of the ordinary. The deputy brushed back his tobacco-colored hair, which had been mussed slightly where his flat-topped brown Stetson had perched. He held the hat in his hand this morning as he adjusted his sidearm. He wore a brown leather cross-draw rig on his left hip, for his right-handed draw. He favored a six-gun Colt T .44–40 double-action with a five-inch barrel and the front sight filed off.

Longarm sat on the varnished bench and picked up the *Gazette.* He'd just become interested in a story when Billy Vail's door popped open and the shorter man stood there staring at Longarm.

"You're late, Longarm. Come on in." Billy turned and stalked into his office, leaving the door open. He dropped into the big chair behind his cluttered desk and frowned. Longarm ambled in, looked around, and sat in the Moroccan red leather chair beside the desk. The banjo clock on the wall showed that the time was 9:15 A.M.

"You don't want to know how many politicians are sending me telegrams about this case," Billy said, his voice loaded with resentment and agitation. "Dozens of them, most from Chicago. It's upset the Washington powers enough that they sent me a wire yesterday telling me to get this thing settled fast.

"They asked for you by name to go on the case to ramrod it, and to pick up whatever help you need in any jurisdiction you might be in."

Billy rubbed his hand across his balding head. His pink face went a shade darker as he turned and looked out the window.

Longarm had not seen Billy so upset in years.

"Then this isn't just a First District Court of Colorado case," Longarm asked, probing.

Billy turned back and picked up an eight-inch-long chipped flint spear point from his desk and let his fingers touch the sections that were flaked away.

"Hell, it isn't even in Colorado yet." He pointed to a folder on his desk with a sheaf of papers clipped to it.

"Started out as a robbery. A daring job done at the Chicago Headliner's Ball. That's the social affair of the year that draws all the biggest politicians in Chicago and the state, and whatever national figures they can get to come. They throw a gourmet dinner and a big fancy dance. All of Chicago's richest society people are there and the most important politicians, who try to raise money for their campaigns."

"Somebody hit that affair?" Longarm asked.

"Not only hit it, cleaned it out. A man and a woman in masks and costumes ripped necklaces and bracelets off women, rings and diamond stickpins off men, stole diamonds, rubies, emeralds, the fanciest jewelry that Chicago society could display. The reports show an estimated value of something over three hundred thousand dollars' worth of loot is missing."

"Uh-oh. Both the Illinois U.S. senators, the governor, all the state officials, and the society snobs." Longarm shook his head. "I can imagine the pressure they generate."

Billy put down the spear point and marched to the window, then came back. "Whatever pressure you can imagine, multiply it by a thousand and you'll be close to it. Here's our file on the case. Mostly telegrams from Chicago and Washington. It's not much.

"The robbers are a man and a woman. He's thirty-five to forty, and she's twenty to twenty-five. She may be a redhead or wear a

5

red wig. They both are slender. They're a known pair of jewel thieves, usually operating by night. We even have their names.

"The man is Eric Heinrich, and the woman is Riane Moseley. No pictures, no sketches, no real descriptions. They're headed our way.

"A police report shows they were seen in Omaha, where they sold two of the gems from the robbery. The diamonds were unset but of the size, color, and shape that matched some of the stolen goods."

"You want me to go to Omaha?"

"No, just hold on and let me finish. Police there identified them, but they slipped through a dragnet and boarded the westbound train."

"Why don't the police down the tracks search the train and grab the pair?" Longarm asked.

Billy scowled and picked up the spear point again. "Because both of them are ex-actors, who are extremely adept at makeup and costuming. They can go on the train young, get off old. They can change their sex with makeup and costuming. They are as slippery as a new caught fish off the hook. Now let me finish.

"Another reported sale of stolen diamonds came from Grand Island, Nebraska, and again they slipped on the train heading west.

"That's as far as we've tracked them. Your job is to get on the Union Pacific train, find the pair, capture them, and recover the gems. Then return the jewels and the robbers to Chicago for prosecution."

"Sounds simple," Longarm said, lighting a cheroot and blowing the smoke toward the ceiling.

"I'm not in the mood for humor," Billy Vail said. "There's a lot at stake here, not only the amount of the stolen goods, but the anger and power of the political figures affected. They want the pair captured quickly."

Longarm sobered. "When were they last seen in Grand Island?"

"Yesterday. Sometimes they spend two or three days in a town, sometimes they jump off, sell a diamond, and catch the next train west."

6

"That would set up North Platte, Julesburg, then Cheyenne, if they keep going west," Longarm said. "They sell the gems to a local jewelry store at well below market price?"

"Yes. Most of it is in the briefing papers. Henry typed up a fresh copy for you so you don't have to strain your eyes. He's working on your vouchers and travel orders. The chief marshals down the rail line will all have been notified about the problem and about you coming into their territory—if you get that far."

"I'll go to Cheyenne this afternoon and talk to the jewelry store owners. Let's just hope that the robber pair has not decided to ride straight through to San Francisco."

Longarm took the file and began reading. The pair had been traveling actors until they branched out into better-paying work. They had been charged with grand theft and armed robbery in two states but not convicted. Now they were wanted in at least ten states and by the federal government.

Longarm dug into the wires and reports. He came to the most factual material yet. The woman stood five-foot-three, and the man five-ten. That could be a help. Disguises seldom changed a person's height.

An hour later, Henry came in with the travel money, vouchers, and his letter from Billy Vail to other chief United States marshals down the tracks.

"If you pack a bag, you can make the twelve-oh-five out of the station," Henry said.

Longarm shot him a reproachful glance. "Might at that, the Lord willing and the creeks don't rise."

"Good idea, Longarm. Get up to Cheyenne as soon as you can. Give you more time to get ready for them."

"If they aren't in Salt Lake City already," Longarm said. What a crazy case. No real descriptions of the prime suspects, who might or might not be selling diamonds as they fled across the country on the transcontinental railroad. All he had to do was catch them and take the desperadoes back to Chicago. Oh, and find the missing $300,000 in precious gems. Sounded so easy it surprised him that the secretary of of the treasury specifically asked for him.

At Denver Longarm caught the branch-line train bound for Cheyenne and the Union Pacific road. He settled down to read. He had to eat this apple a bite at a time. He read the rest of the

7

material before the train pulled into the Cheyenne, Wyoming Territory, station.

By the time he stashed his traveling bag in the Cheyenne Concord Hotel, he was convinced that he had a job that couldn't be done quick or easy. Thirteen hundred miles of railroad tracks separated Denver from San Francisco.

The Chicago jewel robbers could step down at any half-mile marker between here and there and be safe for the rest of their lives. The only chance in Hell he had of finding them depended on how greedy they were and how many of the gems they tried to sell.

Five minutes later, Longarm walked down the snowy Cheyenne street. A few flakes of white still fell from an earlier storm. He brushed away the flakes and stopped at the first jewelry store he found, a block over from the tracks, on the town's main thoroughfare.

He showed his identification and told a capsule story of the robbers and the chase.

"Be right glad to get in touch with you if any strangers come in wanting to sell diamonds," the store owner said. He was a small man with slicked-down hair and a mustache, who smelled of rose water and bay rum. "You say you're staying at the Concord?"

Longarm went to the street again, stepping through six inches of snow on the boardwalk as he looked for the next jewelry store.

Within the next hour, he found six more stores in Cheyenne and two shops that sold jewelry as well as dishes and fancy women's clothes. He worked them all, his story becoming shorter and more concise with each telling.

From the last store, Longarm hurried down to the station and found out the next train came in from the east at five-thirty.

He checked in with the county sheriff, a man named Hoyt Adams. The sheriff's belly overflowed his tan pants. His tan shirt bulged remarkably at his midsection, and his face was fleshy and soft white. The sheriff checked Longarm's identification, then handed it back.

"Yep, seen them before. Most marshals around here come outta Laramie. Chief Marshal Lazarus Benoit is set over there since that's the state capital. Think this pair of robbers will stop here?"

8

Longarm nodded. "My guess is they'll hit the larger towns, sell what diamonds they can and get out of the place fast."

"You don't know what they look like?"

"No, sir, Sheriff. They're actors, wear makeup and costumes, so they might be older than for real. The man could even dress up like a woman."

"Son, sounds like you bought yourself one heap of trouble. Don't know what we can do to help."

"You could send a pair of deputies to the train station in case I spot anybody who looks suspicious. That's for the five-thirty westbound."

"We can do that. Sounds like this pair is pretty smart. How much loot did you say they stole?"

"Over three hundred thousand dollars' worth, most of it from highly placed political and high-society figures in Chicago and Illinois."

Sheriff Adams laughed. His face squeezed up and he chuckled, making his whole body bounce. "Yessireee, young man, you picked out a damn hard pair of steers to get behind the barbed wire. Glad it's not my job. I'll send two men with stars to the depot on time."

Longarm legged it over to the jewelry stores again. He walked the circuit, stopping at the Cheyenne Jewelers. The small man behind the counter nodded when Longarm came in.

"Ain't seen nobody looking to sell," the man said. "I don't buy much from folks. Oh, I do when I know them. Old Mrs. Rielly died last month, and her son sold me two of her rings. Diamonds weren't that big, but they were bright blue whites. Man's got to know his diamonds. Look for clarity, cut, color, and of course ones with no flaws. You say these stolen ones will probably be unmounted?"

"Yes. They'll pull the diamonds out, mash up the settings, and sell the gold to some other jeweler."

A young man came in then looking for a diamond ring for his intended. He settled on one for thirty-five dollars. Longarm figured that was the young man's wages for a month. He waved at the jeweler and went out the door, toward the next store that sold diamonds. His pocket watch showed four-thirty, an hour before the westbound train came in. He'd be waiting.

On his second tour of the stores, Longarm stopped short when he looked in the third establishment. A small, older woman had spread out five unset gems on a velvet pad on the counter, and the jeweler was examining one under his glass.

Longarm entered the store without a sound and checked his Colt in leather. Ready. He stepped up beside the little old lady and cleared his throat.

The jeweler looked up and nodded. "Yes, Mr. Long, nothing to report."

Longarm stared down at the elderly woman. She appeared to be about the right size. The transformation could have been made by a good actress with makeup.

"Oh, Longarm, I'd like you to meet Mrs. Ida Greer. She's a little short on funds right now. I've known Mrs. Greer for fifteen years or more."

Longarm nodded. "Good to meet you, Mrs. Greer." He nodded at the merchant. "I'll be around later on."

She could have been the one. The right size, age could be changed. But she wasn't. Damn. He left the store and moved on to the next one. No customers inside. The jeweler said he'd had no one around selling diamonds.

Longarm disliked this kind of assignment. Lots of footwork, no sure chance to find the crooks, let alone catch them. That along with all the pressure from Chicago and Washington, D.C., was enough to put any man on the defensive.

He watched a pretty red-haired woman come out of a ladies' wear shop and move down the boardwalk ahead of him. Now that perked up his spirits. She looked about the right size, and had red hair. She could be the Chicago jewel thief. Longarm walked faster.

The way her round little bottom twitched when she marched down the street brought a smile to the lawman's face. Could she be the jewel robber? He'd follow her and see.

Six stores down, a man stood from a chair propped up against a storefront. He hurried out to meet the redhead, kissed her cheek, and helped her into a farm wagon with a spring seat. In back were two boxes of supplies and two red-haired little boys.

Longarm paused a moment and looked at the woman. Pretty as a newborn foal. She smiled at him; then the wagon lurched ahead and the man drove down the street.

The U.S. deputy marshal snorted. Well, for a few minutes he'd thought she might be the robber. He heard a train whistle in the distance and hurried toward the red-roofed depot. Maybe he'd have better luck with the people who got off the westbound.

Chapter 2

Longarm leaned against a baggage cart as he waited for the train to arrive in Cheyenne. He wore a long overcoat and gloves for protection against the near freezing temperature. A few patches of snow remained from the last storm, a week ago.

The train came in a little fast, and the sparks flew from the wheels as the men turned down the brake rods, bringing the screech of steel against steel.

The steam engine led the way, snorting and puffing and emitting one last gush of black smoke from its stack as it slowed the two passenger cars and string of eight boxcars. The brakes locked and a gush of steam hissed from the escape valve as the big iron horse shuddered to a stop.

A dozen people hurried off the first passenger car, and a moment later about thirty more streamed off the second car.

Longarm systematically checked and categorized each passenger. From the front car, he quickly spotted a young woman in her twenties, who was slender, no more than five-three, and walked with a decidedly assured attitude. She had short black hair and wore no hat. No one else there could have been the woman robber.

About the same time, he spotted a man off the second car who looked five-ten, about thirty-five years old, and carried a single, expensive traveling case.

Longarm hurried after the woman. She held only one bag and hailed a cab at the edge of the wide boardwalk in front of the station.

"The New Wyoming Hotel, Driver," the woman said as she settled into the rig.

Longarm turned away, searched until he saw the thirty-five-year-old man striding down the boardwalk, and followed him. Two blocks later the man checked in at the New Wyoming Hotel.

When the suspect left the desk, Longarm hurried up and spotted the man's name in the register. It wasn't Eric Heinrich, but he hadn't expected it to be. He reached out and tapped the clerk on the shoulder.

"A young woman just registered a few moments ago. Pretty girl, short dark hair. What room did you assign her?" Longarm held out his deputy U.S. marshal identification, and the clerk gulped and then showed him the register behind the counter. She was in room 210. The man who had just signed in was in 212, right next door.

"Thanks," Longarm said. "Oh, do those two rooms have a connecting door inside?"

"No, not set up as a suite," the clerk said. "We do have two rooms that do."

Longarm nodded and went up the steps three at a time. Down the hall on the second floor, he could see no one. The marshal paused in front of room 210 and heard a woman singing softly. At room 212 he heard a chair being pulled across the floor. They were still in their rooms. He might have them spotted, but he could do nothing about it. Say they were the jewel robbers, he had no evidence that would allow him to break into their rooms and search their baggage.

He leaned against the wall at the end of the hall and waited. After an hour, neither of the two had left the rooms. Longarm's feet hurt, and now his stomach began to growl. Didn't these people eat supper? He left his lookout and walked down the stairs.

Outside, Longarm blew his breath into the night air and watched the moisture condense into a white cloud. It would be cold tonight, far below freezing. He put on his gloves and walked a half block down the street. Just before Longarm stopped at a

13

restaurant, he noticed the lights still on at one of the jewelry stores. He continued to the store and pushed open the unlocked door. He saw the owner of the store grinning.

When the jeweler saw Longarm, his grin faded and he frowned.

"Damn, I might have done something wrong. I bought two diamonds this afternoon. I know, I know, you were here twice and warned me." The man gave a long sigh, scrubbed one hand over his face, and waved. "Come take a look. This slick deal I pulled made me lose all track of my senses.

"Two beautiful blue whites, not a sign of a flaw. The best-quality diamonds I ever seen. Clarity, color both great and not a hint of a flaw, just beautiful."

The jeweler reached under the counter and took out a small box. He opened it and pushed it under a nearby lamp. The diamonds lay on a black velvet liner. They probably weighed a carat each, gleaming and sparkling, reflecting the lamp light.

"Look at the quality of those stones!" the jeweler gushed.

"I see it," Longarm said, his voice low, even. "Who did you buy them from?"

"A little old lady. She must have been seventy-five. Had a whispery voice. Said she had to get enough money for a train ticket to New York."

Longarm tensed. "Are you sure she was old?"

"Sounded like it. Had more wrinkles than I've seen in a long time. Wore gloves, but she had face wrinkles and lines, eyes kind of sad."

"She have on a hat, scarf, big coat?"

"Sure, it's winter out. Must be near freezing out there. You're wearing a coat and gloves."

Longarm nodded. He pulled off his gloves. "How did she walk? Did she move like an old woman, slow and with some pain evident?"

"No, she walked . . . Oh, God. She walked young. When she left here, she pranced out. She moved like a young girl. You mean, I bought diamonds from that robber, the stolen ones?"

Longarm nodded. "Sounds like you might have." From his jacket pocket he took out a list of the loot and under diamonds

14

found listed twenty-five different one-carat diamonds in rings, earrings, and necklaces.

"I can't prove they're part of the stolen diamonds; otherwise I'd confiscate them. What color hair did this old woman have?"

"Hair? Gray, almost white."

"Probably a wig. Eyes, what color were her eyes?"

"Oh, they were blue, light blue. I noticed that. I thought older folks' eye pigment fades. Oh, damn, I guess it probably does."

"How much did you pay for the two stones?"

"Two hundred dollars," the jeweler said, his voice low. "About half what they're worth. I thought I made a great buy."

"You did. What time did she come in?"

"About six o'clock. I was ready to close up when she came in. Since then I've been working and dreaming about a new shop."

"Is there a night train that stops here?"

"Nope. A freight usually goes through east, but it don't stop, just one long string of empty boxcars."

"Next train out heading west?"

"Not until little after seven in the morning, if she's on time. Don't try to set your watch by that morning mixed train."

Longarm stared at the jeweler a moment, then headed out the door. Two more stolen diamonds had been sold. No doubt of it, but he couldn't prove it. Unmounted diamonds didn't have identification numbers. The robber pair should have plenty of money now to get to the coast. They must not be selling the stones for expense money. They were starting to unload them for profit.

Longarm pulled on his gloves and put his coat collar up high. He scowled, thinking about the man and woman in the hotel. The two he had been watching couldn't possibly be the jewel robbers. They were in their rooms during the time the "old" woman had sold the stones, about six o'clock.

Angry with himself for watching a cold fire, Longarm went to the four other largest hotels in town and talked to the room clerks. He showed his identification and quizzed them about a pretty young woman who must have registered early this morning or the day before. He told them her height and described her beautiful pale blue eyes.

15

None of the clerks could remember registering such a woman, and none knew if any such woman was now a guest in his hotel. Longarm fumed all the way through his less than wonderful steak dinner at the Prime Rib restaurant. Back at his hotel, Longarm found out from the desk clerk that the first westbound train left the station at 7:05 A.M.

He sat in the lobby for ten minutes. What would he do if he'd just taken in two hundred dollars from some sold loot? Celebrate. Yes, but how?

The woman would probably leave her makeup on for the morning getaway train ride. It probably took her an hour to put on the disguise. The man would play some poker or do some drinking. He had a woman, so that wouldn't be his call. Longarm hurried out of the hotel and worked the saloons. He checked four of the biggest ones quickly, watching for a man about thirty-five, slender and five-ten.

He didn't find one until the fifth saloon. The man played poker at a table toward the rear. He seemed right, well dressed, and he had a mustache that looked like one actors could take off and put on in a few seconds.

Longarm asked the bartender who the man was.

"Guy with the thin mustache?" the apron asked. "That's Will Pride. He's a regular in here. Plays cards almost every night. Some say he's a professional gambler. Been around town for three or four months now."

If Pride had been here three months, he couldn't be the robber. Longarm thanked the bar man and kept looking.

Two hours later he gave up, finished his draft beer at the bar, and headed for his hotel.

This would be a great time for a sex-starved widow to bang on his hotel door and demand some action. That was too much to hope for. He compromised by reading through the descriptions and known facts about the robber couple again.

They had been traveling as husband and wife, but were often seen apart. Usually they did not sit together on the same train car. Frequently they would change their appearance during a train ride. The woman could get on the train as one person and emerge at her stop as another person entirely.

16

Heinrich had a reputation as a compulsive gambler. In earlier days he would gamble on anything except the sunrise.

Longarm reread one of the items about the woman. "Riane Moseley, 24, trained as a dancer and singer as well as an actress. She once said her ambition was to dance and sing in her own show in the best music halls in New York and Chicago."

A dancer and a gambler. He should be able to make something out of that. If he were a gambler and on this run, where would he play cards? Not in a public saloon. He'd invite the best in town to his hotel room for a private game.

Longarm left his hotel on the run. He found the man he had spotted before, who the apron had described as one of the best gamblers in town, Will Pride. The card game had just broken up.

Longarm walked into the group and stared at the gambler with the string tie and fancy red checkered vest.

"What?" the gambler asked.

"Just wondered if you knew where there was some real action in this one-horse town?"

The gambler looked around and shrugged. "This wasn't bad. The boys here taught me how to play the game tonight." He laughed softly. "Course I won, so maybe I taught them."

"Isn't there some private action here somewhere?" Longarm asked.

The gambler moved closer and motioned Longarm to one side. He and Longarm left the tables and stood next to the back wall.

"Don't know you, stranger. Private games are private, but the one on tonight is a bit short on players. If you want in for three hundred, I'll vouch for you. It's an anything-goes game with all guns checked at the door. That means there may be a pat-down to watch for hideouts and knives."

"Fine, I'm tired of this penny-ante stuff. What time and where?"

"Right now and with me. What's your name?"

"Long."

"I'm Will Pride mostly from Abilene."

"I'm mostly from Denver."

"Passing through?"

"Heading west in the morning. Like to take some Cheyenne money with me."

They left the saloon, reacted to the falling temperature by buttoning their overcoats, and headed down the main avenue.

"We going to the game or is this just a walk for our health?" Longarm asked.

"Going to the game. The New Wyoming Hotel. New gent in town talked to three of us. He said if we saw some good money to bring it along."

"How old is this cardsharp?"

"Thirty-five, maybe more. Smooth as a piece of velvet. I'd guess he knows every cheating move in the book."

"Then why are you playing?"

"If I can't cheat better than he does, then he deserves to win. It's a sporting proposition and nobody gets killed. I finally figured out it's damn hard to win at poker when you're dead. That's why I never carry a gun anymore."

Five minutes later they stood in front of room 323 on the third floor of the New Wyoming Hotel. Will knocked. The door opened to a haze of tobacco smoke.

Three men looked up from where they sat at the table. A fourth man stood beside the open door and stared at Longarm.

"A visitor?" the doorkeeper asked.

"Gent's name is Long, said he's looking for some action," Pride said.

The man stared at Longarm. "You got any cash with you?"

"Three hundred is the stake, I hear," Longarm said.

"Up front, table money, no new cash in the game after it starts," the doorman said. He had a full black beard and mustache. Longarm tried to figure if he wore a stage beard or a real one. The man's dark hair was bushy and curly, a good type to be a wig. The bearded man nodded.

"Let's give it a try. We've been waiting for you to start."

There was no check for weapons. They sat down at the table and the game began. Longarm had played poker like this before. It was hard-driving, no quarter given, and every man for himself. He watched whenever the bearded man dealt. The first time he lost the hand. The next two hands he dealt, he won.

Longarm bet conservatively to stay in the game. He won two pots out of the first ten and came out fifty dollars ahead. The bearded man took the cards next, and Longarm watched the dealer's hands. The man had fantastic fingers and used them to bottom deal. Longarm spotted it.

He sat beside the bearded man at the table. The dealer dealt cards to himself after opening on five-card draw. Longarm's right hand stabbed at the dealer and pinned his hand to the table with a faceup card halfway off the bottom of the deck. It was an ace.

"What the hell?" the bearded man barked.

"I'd say the same thing," Longarm said with a soft yet deadly tone. "What's that ace of spades doing coming off the bottom of the deck?"

"Damned if he ain't right," the man sitting on the other side of the dealer spat. He pushed back his chair, and a hideout appeared in his hand. "We don't cotton to cheaters around here, stranger. Best if you just let go of the cards, ease up from your chair, and back toward the door."

The bearded man's cheeks over his beard flushed; his eyes flashed fury. He stared at the man with the derringer, then slowly rose.

"Hands on top of your head," the gunman said.

"What about my winnings?" the bearded man asked.

"No winnings. In our town a cheater loses. You're damned lucky to be alive, way I look at it. You want to gamble three hundred dollars that I can't hit you with two shots from this little .45?"

The bearded man gave a long sigh, shook his head. "I back out the door?" he asked.

"Not a chance," the man with the gun said. "Bill, split up the money the man has in front of him. Cut it five ways and add it to each of our stacks of cash on the table. Then we'll get out of here and let this one stew in his own juices awhile."

"We should castrate the bastard," one of the men at the table said.

"Hell no, we break both his thumbs," said another man, who was big enough to do it. "Ever see a card slick try to play poker with both thumbs bandaged up?"

19

"You wouldn't do that," the bearded man spat. "Every man at this table has cheated at cards. You just weren't caught."

The man directly across from the cheater stood, drew, and fired a .44 slug into the gambler's right arm so quickly no one could stop him. The bearded man jolted backward two steps and screamed in outrage.

"Enough of that, Shorty," the man with the derringer said. "Split up the cash. Let's get out of here."

Longarm looked at the wound that bloodied the man's upper arm. He took a big handkerchief from his pocket, pulled the gambler's kerchief from his jacket pocket, and made a pad of them. He tied the kerchiefs around the man's arm tightly enough to stop the bleeding.

"Doc Caruthers lives down two blocks on Main you want to find him," the derringer man said.

By that time, the money had been divided and pocketed, and the men stood. They left the room quickly. Longarm stared hard at the gambler, then reached up and jerked at the black beard. It was real.

Longarm shrugged. "Looks like I found the wrong man. Sorry about this, but if you want to live a long time in the West, you've got to learn to bottom deal so it isn't so easy to catch you. If you want to stay alive cheating, I'd advise you to learn your trade." He turned and walked out of the room.

The bearded man held his arm, glaring at Longarm. "I'll see you again, cowboy. When I do, you better have your gun hand ready, because I'll be hunting you down and I'll kill you."

Chapter 3

Longarm walked away from the New Wyoming Hotel a hundred dollars richer but with the stinging threat of the gambler in his ears. He'd heard it all before, but he would be careful the rest of the night and when he got on the train. Chances were the gambler could be on the same westbound.

For just a moment Longarm hoped that his hotel had the newfangled steam heat piped into each room. It was being done more and more now, but he knew that this place didn't have it. When Longarm walked into the lobby, he went at once to a glowing coal-burning stove. It had attracted half a dozen guests, who were trying to get warm enough to rush up to their cold rooms and frosty beds. This would be an excellent time to have a sleep-in lady partner.

Longarm warmed his hands for a moment over the coal fire, then walked up to his room and went through his usual checks to be sure no one waited inside for him. He went in, locked the door, and peeled off his overcoat and gloves, then tugged off his boots. He dove into bed fully clothed and pulled up the blankets. The bed already had three comforters on it, and before morning he wished there were more.

Longarm knew he would not oversleep. He awoke early, packed his one bag, and arrived at the train station by 6:30. He had half a breakfast inside him and a small sack of sweets to nibble on during the fifty-mile trip down the rails to Laramie. With any luck at all, they should arrive there in about an hour and a half. He'd check to see if the Union Pacific's brag about the thirty-five-miles-per-hour average speed between stops held up.

No one noticed him as he sat down on a bench at the near side of the station to wait for the train. It would be coming in from the east, which meant there could be a delay.

He was right. The 7:05 pulled away from Cheyenne promptly at 8:15. The conductor claimed a snowstorm had held them up. Now the tracks were clear, the sky a high, deep blue, and the weather so crisp Longarm's nose burned.

He checked all of the passengers as they boarded the train. None of them answered the descriptions he searched for, but that didn't surprise him. He watched for a little old lady and found one, but she had a thirteen-year-old girl with her and evidently suffered from blindness.

Longarm walked through the first passenger car and inventoried every face again as the train pulled out of the station. He found no one suspicious.

A half hour later, he moved to the second car and scanned the people there. He saw one old, slender man. A possibility, but he had no beard and his face held several sores. The old man refused to look anyone in the eye, and Longarm wrote him off the list.

At last he decided a smart couple running from the law wouldn't get out of town on the first train after the diamond sale in Cheyenne. They would wait for two or three trains, so it would be harder to find them. He knew another train came through Cheyenne heading west about noon.

At least this way he would be in the territorial capital before the jewel thieves arrived and have a chance to do some groundwork with the jewelers. He would bring up the threat of federal prison for them if they didn't cooperate with him. That usually worked.

The train arrived at Laramie at 9:45. Longarm made his first stop at the small federal building, where the second district court of Wyoming Territory had its offices. Longarm knew the chief marshal, Ambrose J. Clapshaw.

The small man, a former army major during the Civil War, now ran the best operation west of the Mississippi, next to Billy Vail's.

22

Longarm went in past the gold-leaf-lettered door and nodded at the clerk, a young lady with soft brown hair and the prettiest smile he'd seen all day.

"Is Marshal Clapshaw in? Deputy Marshal Custis Long from Denver."

"Yes, I remember you from a year ago, Marshal Long. I'm Priscilla Young. I'm sure he's not that busy." She stood and walked to the door with a small movement of body parts that showed up fetchingly under her tight-fitting skirt. She knocked, opened the door, and announced the marshal from Denver.

He touched her shoulder as he passed, and they smiled; then he saw U.S. Marshal Clapshaw knocking an inch-long ash off his cigar.

"Longarm, been expecting you. Just heard about the diamond buy in Cheyenne. Looks like our diamond snatchers are heading this way."

They talked for twenty minutes about how best to nail the pair.

"We've notified all jewelry stores in town, six of them as I recall. We've asked for their cooperation to notify us if anyone comes around offering diamonds or other rare gems for sale. Buying precious gems is not the ordinary situation for our jewelers here in Laramie."

When their talk was over, Longarm asked for two local deputies to be assigned to work with him on the case. Clapshaw gave him one; the others were out in the field on other business, he said.

The deputy's name was B.R. Jarin, he was twenty-three years old and had a year's duty at Laramie. B.R. was short and chunky, had a slight lisp, and wore a gunbelt tied low. Marshal Clapshaw told Longarm that B.R. Jarin had the fastest draw of all his deputies.

"B.R., you know about this case?" Longarm asked.

"Yes, sir. Diamonds. I went around and warned the jewelers about the problem."

"Good, B.R. Let's take the run again. We've got to make these people understand they're our only hope to catch the robbers."

The first jewelry store operated in half of a store formerly used as a saddle shop, and the smell of leather still permeated the place. The store contained three fancy glass cases that showed off a variety of gems, stones, and jewelry.

Longarm met the gaze of the man behind the counter. He showed the jeweler his badge, and the merchant nodded. He dressed well, had his hair combed neatly, and wore half glasses perched on the end of his nose.

"Yes, the marshals told me about the stolen diamonds. I told B.R. here that I'd cooperate."

Longarm smiled. "That's good. Mr. Grimbach, is it? I have a little stronger message. We not only want your cooperation, we want your active help. If anyone comes in who isn't local and you don't know and tries to sell a diamond or other precious stone, I want you to delay them, stall them somehow and send word to Marshal Clapshaw's office. When you do that, we'll get a man right over here and talk to the person trying to make the sale."

Grimbach frowned. "You mean I don't have the right to buy diamonds from whoever I please?"

"Not this time, Mr. Grimbach. If you buy a stolen diamond or ruby or emerald, and we prove it came from the robbery goods, you will be charged with aiding and abetting the robbers, receiving stolen goods, and any other charges we can think of. That would mean four to six years in the territorial prison. You don't want that, do you, Mr. Grimbach?"

"Heavens, can you do that?"

"We certainly can. No matter how innocent your actions might be, receiving stolen property is a felony, with a prison term attached. It doesn't matter whether you know the items were stolen or not. We want to make sure that you don't suffer that problem."

B.R. nodded. "Besides that, Mr. Grimbach, you want to do your civic duty and help us arrest those robbers, don't you? They stole over three hundred thousand dollars' worth of gems back in Chicago."

Sweat popped out on Grimbach's brow. "Heavens, I bought some gems yesterday, all rings and a broach—"

Longarm cut him off. "Mr. Grimbach, that's entirely legal. The people we are after probably weren't even in town yesterday. What we want to do is make certain that if they try to sell any gems here, we have a chance to catch them."

24

Grimbach put away the tray of rings and the broach. "Well, now I see what you mean. Yes, certainly. Unless I know the person is a local, and have had business with them before, I'll make sure to notify Marshal Clapshaw about any potential seller."

"Good, Mr. Grimbach. Chances are they'll pass up Laramie and go on down the tracks, but we have to be ready in case they stop here. Oh, these people are excellent at disguise and makeup. If someone a bit strange shows up, be especially watchful of them."

Longarm and B.R. left the store and moved to the next one.

"Hey, you really turned up the pressure back there, Marshal. You want us actually to threaten these people with prison if they buy a diamond from the robbers?"

"Not my doing, it's the law, B.R. You know that. Now all we have to do is scare the rest of the jewelers half to death and sit back and wait. That and meet the train that must get in here about one-thirty."

They made the rounds, found cooperation from all of the jewelers, who wanted nothing to do with a felony charge. After a sandwich at a cafe, they waited for the train to pull in.

"Remember, they might be anyone. Watch for an old woman, five-foot-three, who walks like a young girl. I have no idea what the man might be dressed as, maybe a tall, slender woman."

When the steamer pulled in at the station, more than fifty people dropped off the two passenger cars. Longarm knew he hadn't been able to get a good look at everyone, even though he'd stood near the station doors and most of the passengers had walked past him.

He spotted one man he figured could be a suspect, but the man met a woman and five kids on the platform. After the rush subsided, he and B.R. stood there watching dozens of backs in heavy coats walking away.

The weather turned a little warmer, up to forty degrees, Longarm noticed, as they passed an outdoor thermometer. They checked in with the county sheriff. He had been briefed by Marshal Clapshaw, but had no new ideas.

Longarm decided that B.R. should wait at the marshal's office in case one of the jewelers tried to get in touch with them. B.R. went back there and came running out at once.

"Henderson Jewelers over on Grand has an older woman trying to sell two diamonds," B.R. called. They hurried over two blocks to the store.

Inside, Longarm saw a small gray-haired woman sitting in a chair. The jeweler, Henderson, worked on a setting at his bench. He glanced up and nodded at the woman. Longarm went to her and paused until she looked at him.

"Ma'am, could I see the diamonds you're trying to sell?"

"Of course, young man. My Harry died three days ago, and I need some money to pay for his funeral. Don't know what all the fuss is about."

She stood and put two diamond rings on the counter. The settings were old and worn, but clean. Each of the diamonds was about a quarter of a carat. None that small was listed among the stolen gems.

"Do you have any identification?" Longarm asked.

"Well, I usually don't carry much to tell who I am, but I do have two letters from my sister in Omaha that just come this morning. Here."

She pulled two letters from the pocket of her heavy coat and gave them to Longarm. They were both addressed to Mrs. Thelma Lowridden, 142 South First Street, Laramie, Territory of Wyoming.

Longarm showed the letters to the jeweler. He nodded.

"Oh, yes, the Lowriddens. Now I recognize her. She hasn't been in here for a while. Her husband did die a few days ago. Sorry about the mix-up."

"Not a problem. Glad you called us. If you get any more sellers you don't know, send another note."

Longarm went back to the woman. "Mrs. Lowridden, I'm sorry about the mix-up. I'm sure that Mr. Henderson will be glad to talk to you about buying your rings."

"Well, it's about time." She got to her feet with a groan and walked over to the counter.

Outside Longarm and B.R. conferred.

"Better to err on that side than the other way," Longarm told the marshal. "I'll make a circuit of the jewelers; you wait back at the office. We might get lucky yet. I had a feeling that the

26

couple we're hunting for came in on that noon train; we just didn't catch them."

It was nearly two hours later, on his second circuit of the six jewelry stores, that Longarm watched as an elderly woman shuffled into the Laramie Jewelry Store. The marshal walked past; then when the woman had made it to the counter and spoken with the owner, Longarm slipped in the store without a sound.

She was just over five feet tall, with a heavy woman's coat that came almost to the floor. She wore a large felt hat and a pair of dark-frame spectacles. Her shoes were old, scuffed, and sturdy. What he could see of her face was sallow and wrinkled.

Longarm examined a case of gold-filled railroad watches at the end of the counter near the window. The woman fumbled for something in her reticule.

"I know it's a shame when a person has to sell a family diamond, but sometimes it happens," the owner of the store, Jacob Nadal, said.

Longarm couldn't hear the woman's response. She laid two cut and polished but unset diamonds on the heavy green cloth atop the glass case. Nadal looked at them, then picked up one and studied it with his jeweler's glass.

"That's a fine stone, brilliant. A fine white and clear. How much do you want for it?"

The woman mumbled something.

"Let me check it down by the window in the better light," Nadal said.

He stopped across the narrow display case from Longarm, his back to the woman. "I don't know her," the jeweler whispered. "She doesn't act like an old lady. Shall I buy?"

"Buy one, then I'll follow her," Longarm whispered, his back to the woman as he looked over a new watch and chain. "She could be the one." Longarm felt his heart race. This was the woman; he knew it. But he needed both of them. All he had to do was follow her back to wherever her accomplice waited, then grab them both and the jewels.

He shrugged. "I'll come back and look at those watches later," he said in his normal voice and strode out the door. On the boardwalk, he moved slowly up the street

27

for twenty feet, then turned and looked in the hardware store window.

He tried to see in the reflection if someone waited in front of the jewelry store for the woman, but he couldn't spot anyone.

Sooner than he expected, the woman shuffled out the door of the jewelry store and to the edge of the boardwalk. A black covered buggy swung down the street and pulled in next to the old woman, who jumped nimbly into the closed rig, which then darted into the street.

"Damn!" Longarm bellowed. He ran after the buggy a ways, saw he couldn't catch it, and looked at the tie rails for a horse. A young man was just tying up his mount. Longarm raced to him.

"Federal lawman, I need your horse," he barked. The young man shook his head.

"Not my Betsy, you don't. I don't want her shot."

Longarm ran to the next horse on the tie rail and got much the same talk. He pulled a twenty-dollar greenback from his wallet, and when he saw a cowboy slide off his mount twenty feet on up the street, he raced there and waved the money.

"Need to borrow your horse. Rent her for this twenty. Right now. I've got to ride."

The cowboy shrugged. "Fine. Bring her back right here." he watched Longarm push back his overcoat and step into the saddle. He charged through Laramie's main street looking for the buggy. Longarm spotted it at the far end of the street leaving town and heading out the North Road.

The buggy picked up speed, and the galloping horse rolled the rig down the trail out of town. Longarm galloped the cow pony for a quarter of a mile and closed the gap, but the black buggy was still three hundred yards ahead of him.

The rig stayed on the road, which forded the creek and vanished behind a screen of trees. Longarm figured the road angled more to the north. He cut across the arc, trying to save time.

Shortly he came to the trees and charged into them. They were thicker than he had figured, and a moment later he had to dismount and walk the animal through the brush. He was almost to the creek when a rifle shot boomed and the lead whispered as it drilled through the air a few feet over his head.

28

Before he could draw his Colt, he saw a shotgun poke out from behind a big cottonwood tree not ten feet in front of him.

"Don't draw that iron or I'll blow you in half," a woman's voice barked at him. He dropped his mount's reins and heard movement behind him. There he saw a rifle barrel aimed at him from around another tree.

"I don't know who you folks are, but I'm a deputy United States marshal on official business. Put down those weapons or you're in big trouble."

A wild, high, screeching laugh came from behind one of the trees.

"Hear that, Babe? This handsome gent says we're in big trouble." It was a second woman's voice that screeched the words.

From near the other tree another laugh. "Oh, hell yes, Gert, we in some hellish big goddamn trouble. We do him here?"

"Can't, Pa heard the rifle shot. Best get him back."

The two women stepped out from the trees. The one on the right wore an old army overcoat and a Russian-type fur hat. Long black hair straggled down her shoulders. It was dirty and matted. The coat looked as if it had been through a hog wallow, twice.

The other woman was younger and had on a dirty brown woman's overcoat and no hat. Her long blond hair was dirt gray and matted, and her nose dripped. Her face and hands looked as filthy as the coat.

"What's going on here?" Longarm demanded.

"Keep your hands high away from that six-gun if'n you want to keep your family jewels. Otherwise I'm gonna blow them off with a shot of hot lead."

"Don't you dare!" the younger one shouted. "I'm first, you hit him in the legs, not his crotch." They both laughed.

"We best get this prize back to show to Pa before he beats on us again."

"You, pretty man," the younger one said. "You march straight up that path over there next to the creek. North a ways and don't dawdle. Babe will bring your mount. Not much of a horse, but reckon you know that."

"Look here, ladies . . ."

The shotgun roared and the deadly load of buckshot whispered over Longarm's head by two feet as Gert let go with one barrel.

"Come on, move. Then I won't have to kill you right here."

Longarm walked up the game path along the stream. Less than a quarter of a mile north, in a heavy patch of brush and cottonwoods, they stopped him at a covered wagon pulled by two fancy mules.

A bear of a man backed out the rear opening of the covered wagon and stepped heavily to the ground.

"What the hell you girls been up to?" he bellowed.

"Out hunting like you told us, Pa," Babe said. "Look what we caught for ourselves."

When the big man turned around, Longarm realized what he'd stumbled into. Rawhiders. The lowest, most murderous kind of outlaw on the Western scene. Most of this kind would kill a man for his horse and saddle. They lived by attacking travelers and out-of-the-way farms and ranches, butchering all the people, stealing everything they could sell in the next town, then burning down the buildings to confuse the local law.

The man wiped his hands on his grease-blackened overalls. He was more than six feet tall and must have weighed nearly three hundred pounds. His bearded face split in a grin.

"By damn, a young man for the old woman," he said.

"No, Pa, you said Gert and me got the next man. You promised."

The rawhider wiped a blackened sleeve over his nose and shrugged. "Hell, why not. The old lady rode into town, won't be back until dark. I'll tie his hands behind him, then you two horny girls help yourself."

He stared hard at both of them. "Just don't kill him. You kill him and I'll slice your tits off clean and proper. You hear me, you two hellions?"

"Yes, Pa," the two young women said almost in unison. Then they cheered and ran for Longarm.

Chapter 4

Longarm felt worse than helpless. The old man had pulled the overcoat off the marshal and kept it. Then he tied Longarm's wrists together securely behind his back. The girls prodded him up the step into the back of the covered wagon. It felt as cold inside as it had outside, but both girls immediately stripped out of their coats and shirts and were naked to the waist before Longarm had a chance to look around.

The inside of the wagon looked like a store, with boxes and sacks of goods. Just what they were, he had no idea. A bed of sorts took up one side of the wagon. The older of the two girls, the dark-haired one, pushed him down on the bed and unbuttoned his jacket, vest, and his shirt until she could rub her hands over his hairy chest.

"Oh, yes, this is going to be a great one," she said.

"It's my turn first," the younger girl whined.

"Shut up and be glad you get a turn. Remember how you messed up the last man we caught."

The dark-haired girl had hand-size breasts, with small pink areolas and dark nipples. She bent and brushed one nipple over Longarm's face, then squeezed his cheeks until he opened his mouth and she lowered her breast into it.

"You bite me hard, I'll smash one of your balls," she whispered. "Just suck me good, chew a little, but nothing that hurts."

Her hands had found his crotch and felt for a hardness she didn't locate. A moment later she had his fly open and worked one hand inside.

"Oh, yes, now that's more like it!" She pulled his pants down and opened the long underwear until she had his erection fully exposed.

Longarm had been searching for some way to escape. He lay on his back, on top of his arms, and it hurt like hell. He analyzed his situation. Obviously after the three women had their fill of him, they would have to kill him. They'd take his clothes and gun and horse and sell them down the trail somewhere.

How could he get an advantage? First he had to cooperate with their frantic lovemaking. Maybe it would give him an edge. If not with the older girl, maybe the younger one. This girl, Babe, looked cleaner where her clothes had covered her. But he'd never even thought about a slap and tickle with a woman so just plain dirty.

Her hand fit around his hardening staff and she stroked it back and forth. For several moments he forgot about trying to escape.

"Oh, now that's the way to do, yes, sir," the girl crooned. "I like them big and hard and ready!"

She sat on the edge of the bed and stripped off the men's pants she wore. She had nothing on under them. The chunky, dark-haired girl had fat thighs and strong legs. She pulled his pants down and off one boot, then spread his legs and knelt on the bed. Longarm shivered from the sharp cold inside the wagon.

The girl glared at him, dirty hair falling over half of her face.

"How does it feel down there looking up? I know how, especially when I didn't want to be there. This is a payback, Big Man. This is a payback for all the men who rape all the women. We hate it. When we want to get sexy and make love, you'll know. Right now I want to hurt you!"

She moved forward and caught his erection, brought her knees up and got to her feet squatting directly over him. She positioned her round bottom, then lowered it toward him and swore softly as he penetrated her. Then she settled down on his shaft as it slid upward into her hot and ready scabbard.

"Oh no, not again!" she wailed. "I start out so strong, then when he gets inside, I kind of melt. Oh, no! Now I want it worse than you do. Damn but I hate this. Why can't I be stronger?"

Longarm lay still, not wanting to set her off on another wild tangent. He heard the other girl laughing.

"Don't mind her none, U.S. Marshal," the younger girl said. "Babe's always this way. Claims she don't like it, but she really loves to get poked. She used to be a whore in Denver."

"Did not!" the girl over him brayed. "Never was a whore. I just went to bed with men I wanted to."

"Whore, whore, whore," the younger girl chanted.

The woman on top of him began rocking back and forth, and soon Longarm couldn't stop his own hips from thrusting to meet her movements. They worked up a tempo and a rhythm, and soon both of them pumped hard and fast, their breath coming in big gulps.

The girl panted and hissed, her body pounding faster now, and she wailed like a long-lost child. Then she stiffened, and every fiber in her body tensed as she jolted into a series of spasms and climaxes that Longarm couldn't count, let alone keep up with. Her hips slammed into him a dozen more times; then she sighed and relaxed. She chanted some words he didn't understand. Before he could move, she jolted into another long series of climaxes, with the final one bringing a scream of satisfaction and victory like Longarm had never heard come from a human female.

She rested only a minute, then lifted off him and furiously pulled on her clothes. She wouldn't look at him. She grabbed her long overcoat and surged out the back of the wagon.

Longarm watched her go, then tried to jump up and reach for his gunbelt, forgetting his hands were bound.

The blond girl caught it first and lifted it away from his grasp.

"You don't need this. If you try to go outside, Papa will cut you in half with double-aught buck."

"Then what can I do? That fat man out there is going to kill me no matter what I try. How can I lose by taking that gun away from you right now?"

33

She frowned a moment. "You're right. A man likes to have a fighting chance. My old daddy taught me that."

"I thought the big bear of a man was your father."

She laughed. "Him? I only been with him for six months. Last summer he come to our little farm. First he shot my daddy right between the eyes; then he raped my mother. She fought him until he killed her. Then he raped my older brother and killed him. He kept me for later, he said. He and his wife stole everything they figured they could sell from our place, then burned it down and scattered our cows. He stole the four horses and sold them in the next town.

"I been with him ever since. Says he'll kill me if I try to get away. He will. It ain't so bad. He pokes me now and then, but I'm still alive. I saw him kill another girl when she tried to run."

"I can help you get away," Longarm said. "If you want to get free of him and lead a normal life again, I can help. Give me my gun and let me get dressed. You get dressed to travel. I'm a deputy United States marshal. I can help you."

"You want to do me first, you know, screw me?"

"That would be fine, but it's more important to get you away from here. Get your warm traveling clothes on and think about it. I'll dress, then you can decide. Where did the other girl go?"

"Babe? She's out for a run. After getting poked so damn good that she bellows, she likes to go out and run through the woods for an hour or so. Cleanses her, she says. But then she's just a whore from Denver."

Longarm watched the girl again, then held his hands out to her. She sighed, lifted her brows, took a knife, and sliced the ropes that held his wrists.

"You sure you'll take care of me, get me some clothes, and a place to stay in town?"

"I'm sure," Longarm said.

She scowled, then nodded.

Longarm slipped into his trousers and buttoned his shirt. Then he tightened his boot laces and reached for his six-gun The girl's hand came down on top of his, then relaxed. She looked at him.

"I never did go along with all the killing. I've seen him kill at least forty people. Good folks, honest, just trying to make a living. He killed them like he'd swat flies."

"Is there a shotgun in here?" Longarm asked.

"Mine." She pointed to one and handed him a half dozen shells. "Buckshot. Better than nothing."

He checked the loads. One round had been fired in the double-barreled weapon. He replaced the round with a new one and snapped the scattergun closed.

"You ready?" he asked.

She'd put on her shirt and two sweaters, then the heavy woman's overcoat. She found the Russian hat and pulled it on, then nodded.

"You about done in there, little Gert?" a voice boomed from outside.

"I get a half hour; you always said a half hour," Gert bellowed.

"Hurry it up. I got me a hankering myself now. Hell, I don't mind being third one on him."

Longarm pointed to the front of the wagon. "Can we get out that way?"

Gert nodded. They climbed over wooden boxes and up to the small hole in the canvas top that led to the driver's seat. Longarm stretched forward and looked out. The sun hadn't set yet. He saw his horse, still saddled, tied to a tree twenty feet from the wagon.

He pulled back. "Gert, you go out the back. Take my six-gun and be sure he sees it. Tell him I'm still tied up. I'll get the horse. Stay well away from him. I'll have the shotgun."

She nodded, took the gunbelt and Longarm's Colt, and headed for the back opening. When she saw Longarm near the front, she bellowed out something and jumped down from the wagon.

Longarm edged out the hole in the front, onto the driver's seat. He had thought of driving the wagon away, but it couldn't go fast enough. He needed the cow pony to ride and to take the girl.

Longarm was concealed from the rawhider by the top of the wagon. He went down the off side, away from the big man. He eased off the seat with one foot on the wagon wheel, trying not to make the rig move. It bounced a little.

35

He could hear the girl talking to the rawhider in back. Longarm had to go around the mules' heads, then go across the open space to get to his horse.

The voices rose to screams behind the wagon. It was a wild argument. He listened.

"You little slut," the rawhider roared. "I fed you for six months and what thanks do I get?"

"You killed my family. You raped me. You want me to *thank you*?"

"Shoulda killed you on the spot," the man said.

Longarm stepped away from the horses. He could see both of them now. They were standing twenty feet apart shouting at each other. He lifted the scattergun and pointed it at the big man. As he watched, the bear of a man drew a derringer from his overalls pocket.

Gert lifted the big .44–40 Colt with both hands and fired. The heavy slug caught the man in the belly and drove him back three awkward steps. He screamed and lifted the derringer.

Gert brought the weapon down from where it had recoiled and fired again. The second slug hit him higher in the stomach. He staggered back two more steps and brought up the derringer again.

Longarm bellowed at the rawhider. "Drop the gun or you're a dead man!"

The big outlaw turned his head and watched Longarm a second, then fired the derringer at the girl.

Gert screamed and fell.

Longarm triggered the shotgun and watched the buckshot riddle the huge frame from thirty feet away. The man brayed and whimpered. The derringer dropped from his hand. He sank slowly to his knees, then toppled on his face on the frozen ground. Longarm watched him. He didn't move.

The marshal ran to the girl. She sat up and pointed to her shoulder. He pulled down the coat and looked at her arm. The slug had penetrated the wool coat, nipped a quarter of an inch of flesh, and exited the coat.

"You'll live," Longarm said. "Did Babe take a shotgun with her?"

Gert nodded. "She always carries one."

Longarm grabbed his gunbelt and strapped it on, then reloaded the two spent shells and holstered the Colt. He caught Gert's hand and ran with her toward the horse.

Babe charged into the clearing from the woods on the far side. She was less than forty yards away. She bellowed in a rage when she saw the big man down and bloody and Longarm free.

"What the hell's going on?" Babe yelled.

"I'm getting out," Gert called. "I'm done with this murdering family."

"Nobody leaves alive," Babe said, lifting the shotgun. "Double-aught buck. I'll splatter you both at once."

Longarm caught Gert, and they both lunged behind the horse.

The shotgun blasted. Longarm felt a stinging in his leg over his boot. It was buckshot, not the far deadlier double-aught. She was too far away for the load to be effective. He leaned around the horse and fired a round over Babe's head.

"You're no relation to this scum," Longarm said. "He's dead. His game is over. You might as well come into town with us."

"No, never!" She blasted the second round from the shotgun, but the buckshot's power was used up before it reached them. Longarm mounted quickly and hauled Gert up in back of him.

In a heartbeat, he kicked the horse into motion and slanted into the brush. Before Babe could reload, they were out of range and riding for town. They soon made it to the road and could see Laramie less than half a mile away.

Snow began to fall—gentle, cold flakes that dusted them with white as they rode.

"You really mean that about helping me get a new start?" Gert asked him.

"How old are you?"

"Almost sixteen. My birthday is the fourth of July."

"Good. I know some people here who will help you. You had much schooling?"

"I can read and write and cipher some. I finished through grade six before we moved. Then not much school after that."

"I think I have just the person to help you."

They rode into town, and Longarm tied up in front of the Federal Building. They shook off the dusting of cold snow, and

37

he took Gert into the main lobby. He sat her down on a wooden bench and said he'd be right back.

Upstairs he went into the U.S. marshal's office, stood in front of Priscilla Young, the marshal's clerk, and smiled.

"Priscilla, you live in a place by yourself as I remember. How would you like a roommate?" He told her the situation. "Gert is fifteen, has seen a lot of the rougher side of life already. Now she needs a big sister to help her finish her schooling and get a good start."

Marshal Clapshaw came out partway through the story.

"Rawhiders in my district? Where? I want a team of deputies out there as soon as possible."

Longarm told him where they were. "The old woman is in town, and the man is dead. There's another girl out there somewhere. Both the women will give you trouble."

Clapshaw snorted and hurried out to find his deputies.

Priscilla told Longarm to bring the girl up to the office. He did, and at once the two seemed to hit it off. Priscilla told Marshal Clapshaw she had to take the rest of the day off, and he nodded, hardly hearing her.

Just before she left, Priscilla frowned at Longarm. "Oh, almost forgot. We had another report of a diamond seller. B.R. looked for you, then went to the store. It's the Lawson Jewelers over on Fourth Street."

Longarm thanked her and hurried toward the jewelry store. The snow had stopped. It had made a light covering on the boardwalk, so each new boot or shoe left an imprint.

When he ran up to the store, Longarm found B.R. and the owner, Ben Lawson, staring at each other over the counter. Lawson looked up and moved down the display cases when he recognized Longarm.

"I sent a message to the office, and I waited for an hour before I finally went ahead and bought the diamond. He was willing to sell it at one quarter of the market price. What was I supposed to do? I waited an hour. No judge in Wyoming will convict me of a felony after I cooperated as much as I did."

Longarm held up both hands.

"Who was the seller?"

"A man in his forties I'd say, mustache and trim Van Dyke beard. He spoke with an educated English accent which he tried to downplay, but I could tell. He said he hoped to get the train to San Francisco to sample that town's atmosphere. Claimed to be a writer and wanted to convey the ambience of San Francisco to his readers in England. Said right now a case of short of funds had caught him. He told me he bought the unset diamond from a wholesaler in New York to give to his wife for their anniversary. But he had to part with it at a bargain to complete his trip. He sounded most distressed."

"You got a name from him, a New York and London address?" Longarm asked.

"Yes, of course. I did all you asked me to do."

"Except to wait for a marshal to check out the man."

"The diamond is on the list, I'm sure, Longarm," B.R. said. "It's a two-carat stone, brilliant cut blue white and flawless. Market value at least four hundred dollars."

"Let me see it," Longarm said. He examined the diamond with the jeweler's glass. "It certainly could be from one of the stolen collections. Describe the man for me. Was he fat, thin? What color eyes?"

"He was slender, well dressed. He had brown eyes; I looked at them to make sure. Cultured, precise, at ease."

"Almost as if he were an actor playing an Englishman?" Longarm asked.

"Well, yes, you could say that. I believed his story. When no one came after an hour of stalling, I at last gave in, counted out a hundred dollars, and bought the stone."

Longarm shrugged. "All right, we aren't going to arrest you. You can relax. We can't prove beyond the shadow of a doubt that the gem you bought is a part of the loot. We believe it to be, but that's not proof enough for a court of law. Thanks for your cooperation."

Outside, B.R. bristled. "You mean we can't arrest him? If he'd waited another five minutes I would have been there. We were hunting you. Damn. I should have gone right over. Where were you?"

Longarm gave him a brief rundown.

"So they must have known you were caught, turned their buggy around, and come back to town, and this time the man did the selling at Lawson Jewelers." B.R. snorted. "You're right. This pair is smart and crafty, and know how to take chances. Think that they're through in Laramie?"

"My guess is that they are. Rock Springs would be the next spot to check. But I'm not sure they'll leave on the next train. They might stay here a day or two to help confuse us, to throw us off their tracks."

"Oh, while you were gone, a young woman came hunting you. She said something about wanting to talk to you about the big jewel robbery in Chicago. Said you could contact her at her hotel if she doesn't find you before supper.

"She's at the Raven's Roost Hotel, half a block down from our office. She said she had an interesting proposition for you. Oh, her name is Kimberly Walkenhorst, and she's in room 203 in the Raven's Roost."

It was dark outside by then. Longarm checked his pocket watch. A minute past five.

"With any luck this woman will be Riane Moseley, the jewel thief herself, and she wants to give up. But chances of that are slim to nowhere in sight. I'll stop by that hotel and see if she's in."

He told B.R. about the chief sending out some deputies to rout out the rawhiders. B.R. hurried back to the office, hoping he could go along.

It started snowing again as Longarm walked to the hotel. Inside the Raven's Roost, he brushed the snow off his overcoat and looked at the key boxes behind the desk clerk. There was no key in the box for room 203. He climbed the steps and knocked on the door. After a brief pause, he knocked again.

The door swung open, and a small, shapely woman stared at him. Then she smiled. She was attractive, had long brown hair with touches of red in it and green eyes. She nodded at him.

"Yes, I'm right. You're Deputy U.S. Marshal Custis Long, better known as Longarm. You're working the great Chicago jewel robbery on special orders from Washington, D.C. Come in. I have some interesting developments on the case I'm sure you'll want to know about."

Chapter 5

Longarm took off his flat-crowned hat and watched the pretty woman who had just invited him into her hotel room.

"You know something about the jewel robbery, miss?"

"I certainly do. Don't you want to know what it is?"

"Probably, miss. But this is your hotel room."

She smiled and motioned inside with her hand. "Mr. Long, it doesn't bother me, if it doesn't bother you. Won't you come in?"

He stepped inside and she closed the door.

"That puzzled expression on your handsome face makes me think you're trying to figure out exactly who I am and what my part in this affair might be. That's why I'm going to tell you. I like everything out front and in the open. Is that all right with you, Longarm?"

"Ayuh, just about what I've been thinking, miss. Who are you?"

She waved him into the room's one, wooden chair, sat on the bed, and tucked one leg under her long skirt. Her blouse was white, and the fabric stretched tight over her breasts. She pushed long brown hair from her face and watched him a moment.

"Marshal Long. My name is Kimberly Walkenhorst, and I represent the Illinois First Insurance Company. As you might have guessed, my firm has insurance on

41

about half of the jewels stolen from that Chicago fancy ball."

Longarm stood and set his hat squarely on his head. "Miss Walkenhorst, I'm a government lawman. We don't interact with civilians on a case. I work alone, but thanks for your kind offer of assistance."

Kimberly took six quick steps to the door and leaned against it.

"Not that easy, Longarm. I haven't come all this way to be tossed aside like a burr under your saddle. Right now I know twice as much as you do about the lost gems, and about the two robbers. Isn't it your duty to gather all of the information you can in your chase after these two?"

"Naturally that's part of my job, but—"

She cut him off neatly. "No buts about it, Longarm. I have valuable information that will help you in this case. You don't even know what I'm asking in return. I might want nothing. How can you know until I tell you?"

"As a general rule—"

She stopped him with an angry glance. "I'm not in the army and I don't like generals, let alone general rules, Mr. U.S. Marshal. Why don't you take off your hat, sit back down, and at least listen to what I have to suggest before you storm out of here like you're insulted and furious because a mere woman has had the gall to offer her help to the big, tough, invincible U.S. marshal?"

Longarm chuckled. "You're a feisty one, ain't you? That's not what I woulda said at all. Fact is I was going to tell you that as a general rule I get little help from people not directly involved on a case, truth be spoke. I'd be pleased to listen to what you can tell me about those two fancy-pants actors. 'Long with any suggestions you might have about how to identify and capture them."

"Oh." She took careful steps back to the bed and sank down on it, her bravado gone. Kimberly lifted her brows. "Well, I guess I got told off in a nice way. Sorry. I get a little worked up sometimes when men don't pay any attention to what I'm trying to do to help them."

She looked up, her face a radiant smile showing even, white teeth. "Am I forgiven for being so abrupt?"

"Nothing to forgive."

"Good. Now I know a lot about the pair of robbers. I'll be glad to tell you what I know; then we can work as a team to track them down, arrest them, and get back the diamonds. That will save my company nearly a hundred and fifty thousand dollars in insurance payments.

"That's about it. I'll contribute everything that I have to go with your information and then we'll work together and catch them."

Longarm stood. "Now, Miss Walkenhorst, you've had your say. Mine is about the same as it was before. I'll be glad to listen to any help you can give the United States marshal's office, but regulations prevent me from working with anyone not in law enforcement. Sorry. Now, do you want to tell me what else you know or not? It's up to you."

Kimberly stood and flounced back and forth, her dark skirt swirling, her breasts pressing hard against the restrictive white blouse. She made one more circuit and then stopped in front of him.

"You want me to give up my one bargaining chip and get nothing in return? How could you ask me to do that? Ridiculous. I'll work on my own. I'm not without friends along the rail line."

Longarm reached down, put his hand on her chin, and turned her face up to his. Slowly, so she could back away if she wanted to, he lowered his lips toward hers. Kimberly didn't move. She stood there and let him kiss her, but didn't respond. When he pulled away, her eyes flashed.

"You think that's going to convince me to tell you what I know?"

"Wasn't thinking about that. When you get mad that way, you're the prettiest lady I've seen in weeks."

She stomped her foot and moved back. "Oh, you men! I don't know why we put up with you. You're saying that in the past weeks you've toured Chicago and Philadelphia and New York and seen a million woman so I should be flattered and fall all over myself and tell you what I know because you said I was the prettiest. Honestly, you have a lot of nerve, U.S. Marshal Custis Long. I'd like you to leave my room. If you don't, I'll start screaming, and a U.S.

43

deputy marshal wouldn't want that, now would he? Out!"

Longarm grinned and moved to the door. He started out and looked back. He was about to say something when she pointed to the door and he left, chuckling as he went. He didn't know what she knew about the robbers, and it might be important. If so, she'd be along on the hunt for them. He figured for sure that he'd see her again here in Laramie or at least down the tracks in Rawlins or Rock Springs.

When he left the hotel, Longarm realized he was hungry. He pulled his overcoat up around his neck, angled across the street to the Bull Moose Cafe, and walked inside. A man at the counter paying for his meal looked up and saw Longarm. The man's hand dropped down next to his low-tied iron, and he turned to face the marshal from fifteen feet away.

"You, fancy dan with the flat hat and the cross-draw rig. I figured I'd run into a yellow belly like you again soon enough. You want to eat lead right here or go out on the street?"

Longarm frowned for a second. Then he remembered—the bottom-dealing gambler from Cheyenne. He had the full black beard, mustache, and curly black hair.

"You still bottom dealing, card shark?"

"Draw, you bastard! Right here, right now, yellow belly. Unless you're scared to draw on me."

Longarm waved at the people in the cafe. "You want to kill half the people here with your wild shots? I've got no argument with you, bottom dealer. I told you if you insist on cheating at poker to learn how to do it well. That's good advice. If you don't want to take it, that's your never mind."

The black-bearded man with the red gambler's vest shook his head. "No chance you're talking your way clear, Gutless. You face me here, or I'll wait until you come outside. Which is it going to be?"

"It's dark outside. Are you that good a shot in the dark?"

"Good enough. We'll stand on the boardwalk where the light spills out of the saloons."

"How old are you?" Longarm asked.

"Huh? I'm thirty-five and it's none of your business."

"You want to live to be thirty-six, you better learn to hold your temper and your gunplay. Otherwise somebody's gonna be faster

44

and shoot straighter than you do. Not a nice way to end a good hand of poker."

"Outside, right now before I start shooting!" the gambler bellowed.

Longarm shrugged, picked up a coffee cup off the table, turned his back on the gambler, and carried the mug to the back wall of the restaurant. He moved a table to one side and stood back twenty feet.

"Who wants to be in a little demonstration?" Longarm asked the twenty people in the cafe. "Nobody gets hurt. Just want you to hold this cup at arm's distance and drop it. Simple." Half a dozen men held up their hands, eager for some excitement. Longarm grabbed one of them, gave him the coffee cup, and positioned him with his side to the back wall of the cafe.

Longarm looked at the bearded one. "Little demonstration for you, gambler man. This gent here is going to hold that cup at arm's length and drop it. I'll draw and shoot and see if I can smash it with a .44 round before the cup hits the floor. You want to try it first?"

The gambler shook his head. "That's a no-win bet. Not a man in a thousand can draw that fast."

Longarm shrugged and faced the man with the cup. He was twenty feet away.

"Drop it anytime you feel like it," Longarm said.

The man lifted his brows, then reached the cup to arm's length. He held it there for a count of five, then let go. It fell straight for the floor.

Longarm's right hand snaked to his left side, drew the Colt .44–40 from leather, and swept it around. In that split second his right thumb cocked the hammer and he pointed and shot. The .44-caliber slug smashed the cup while it was still a foot from the floor. A cheer went up from the patrons. The bearded gambler quickly moved his hands away from his sidearm.

Longarm cocked the hammer again and centered his sights on the gambler's chest.

"Any questions?" the U.S. deputy marshal asked the poker player, whose mouth fell open as his eyes went wide. "Just consider that cup was you, gambler man, and right now you're stretched out on the floor there with a hole the size of a baseball in your heart. Not much fun to think about, is it? You still want to call me out for a shoot?"

The gambler closed his mouth. He glanced around to see how many people had seen the demonstration. He shook his head. "No, sir, gunman, no, sir, I don't want to draw against you. Reckon I'll just get on over to the saloon and practice on my card dealing." He looked up at Longarm. "If that's all right with you, that is."

"Fine with me," Longarm said. "You might even try a streak of honest gambling, just to see how good you are at cards. An expert doesn't need to cheat. He knows the cards, reads the players, and bluffs more than shows. Sorry you're leaving, but it's past time for my supper here in the cafe."

The bearded man left at once. Longarm moved the table back in place and ordered his supper, the biggest steak the cafe offered.

His steak arrived, and he looked up at the waitress. Only it wasn't the young woman who'd taken his order. Kimberly Walkenhorst served him the steak, then brought a smaller one for herself and sat down across from him at the table for two.

"Now, don't get angry. Just because we can't work together on the case is no reason we can't at least be civil to each other. I thought a nice supper together would help."

Longarm, silent since he first recognized her as she brought his dinner, grinned. "I guess it can't be all that bad. Settle in and enjoy your supper."

As they ate, he learned she had been raised in Chicago and that her father was a policeman for the big city. She'd wanted to be a cop as well, but the force didn't hire women, not for any reason. They had four women in headquarters doing paperwork, but Kimberly said she'd rather die than be a secretary.

When the steaks were gone and they worked on cherry pie, Kimberly glanced up at him. "I saw that little set-to with the gambler. Are you always that frank with strangers and that good with your iron?"

"So far, so good," Longarm said. He frowned a moment. "What can you know about the robbers that all the police and sheriffs and our own marshals don't know?"

"I know enough that you should have the information. But

since you won't cooperate with me, there's no chance that I'll tell you what my facts are."

"Even if it means the robbers get to San Francisco and sail for China?"

"Especially then, and especially now when we still have a good chance to catch them." She toyed with a round red cherry on her fork. "Of course I understand that you have no incentive to catch them. It makes no difference whether they get away with this or not to the U.S. marshal's office. You're just doing a job that somebody gave you."

"You do have some incentives?"

She ate the cherry and put down her fork. "Well, yes. I'm not actually working as an employee for the insurance firm. Legally I'm a free-lance investigator for them."

"So you get ten percent of anything that we recover that was insured," Longarm added. "I've heard of such arrangements. Let's see, ten percent of three hundred thousand . . ."

"Well, it wasn't quite three hundred thousand they had insured with this company. More like a hundred and fifty thousand."

Longarm chuckled. "If you recovered the whole bunch, you'd be paid fifteen thousand dollars."

"Well, something like that."

"Big money for a detective. Say a store clerk is getting paid forty dollars a month. Not bad wages. It would take that clerk thirty years to make anywhere near fifteen thousand dollars."

Kimberly grinned. "That's why I'm not a store clerk. Also remember that if I recover nothing, I can claim only my expenses for the entire chase."

"Poor you."

"Don't patronize me, Longarm." Her quick anger faded and she smiled again. The smile dazzled Longarm, which he knew it was supposed to do. "Look, I know that two minds are always better than one. Especially in a puzzle kind of a case like this. There are only so many ways that this team can go. Only so many dodges they can pull and masks and makeup they can use.

"We both know that they are heading for the coast. Just why I'm not sure, and I don't think you are either. They seem to be selling more diamonds than they need to just to meet their expenses. Why? We also know that he's a gambler. I heard

47

about your set-to with William Hardrack back in Cheyenne. That was the name of the bearded gent who just challenged you to a shootout.

"You at last figured out that Hardrack wasn't the jewel robber. You see, I know quite a lot about this caper, and I'm angry with you for not wanting to work with me on it."

"I told you why I couldn't. Your command of the English language, or your hearing, isn't as good as I thought. I can work with local marshals, sheriffs, city police, and other law organizations, but not with private citizens such as the Pinkertons or the Walkenhorsts."

"You told me."

"On the other hand, what if you decided to split your reward right down the middle with me? Seven thousand five hundred for me, seven thousand five hundred for you?"

She stared at him, tiny frown lines showing in her forehead. Kimberly sighed, then held out her hand. "All right, half a roast duck is better than no duck at all."

Longarm grinned and pushed her hand away. "You should know by now that U.S. deputy marshals can't accept any kind of reward, gratuity, or bribe."

She withdrew her hand, a pout showing. "That was sneaky, tricky, and underhanded, Custis Long. I didn't expect that from you."

"It was just a little joke, Walkenhorst. Don't get on your high horse. No reason we have to hate each other. We both have a job to do. It turns out to be the same job. While we can't work together hand in glove, there's no reason that we can't have dinner together now and then and compare notes."

Kimberly's face blossomed with a big smile, and she half stood as she reached across the table and pecked a quick kiss on Longarm's cheek.

"Good! Now you're talking some sense. They hit two stores here today, and you chased them in the buggy. Too bad you didn't have a horse handier. But they won another round. Do you think that they'll try again here in town, or will they move on?"

"Well now, let's eat this apple a bite at a time. They'll leg it on down the tracks, but maybe stay here a day or two to throw off our timing. I need some time in the next town to set up the jewelry store owners. I'll be pulling out on the morning train. It comes through here at five-thirty in the early A.M."

"So early?" Kimberly wailed. "I'm a night person. I work better at night and hate to get up so early. But I guess I'll have to. Save me a seat?"

"Why not. More coffee?" She nodded.

"You think they'll follow the same pattern?"

He closed his eyes. It was a question he'd been asking himself ever since the second jewelry store sale. How could they expand their customer base?

"Ayuh, I think so. Same pattern. Small towns offer a limited number of buyers. The jewelry stores will still be their primary prospects. In some towns the smartest and most affluent men are the men who own and run the banks. I've been thinking of talking to the bankers in the next town."

She nodded. The waitress brought them more coffee. "Sounds reasonable. In a lot of these smaller towns, there's only one bank."

"Fewer bases to cover."

Kimberly sipped her coffee and laughed silently over the rim as she watched him. "If I didn't know any better, I'd say that the two of us were starting to work together on this jewel robbery chase."

"Nothing of the sort," Longarm said. "I'm just checking some facts with an interested civilian. Nothing more."

Kimberly laughed softly and watched Longarm again. "I'm glad we have that cleared up. It rather sets the guidelines." She grabbed the bill the waitress put on the table. Kimberly rose quickly and headed for the woman at the front of the cafe. She paid for the meals and had her change when Longarm caught up with her.

"You're fast on your feet," he said.

"Planned it that way," Kimberly said.

"So that means I owe you a supper. How about tomorrow night in Rawlins?"

"I figured you'd want to skip Rawlins and go right on to Rock Springs."

They put on their overcoats and gloves and walked out into

49

the cold night air. It was well below freezing now, Longarm decided.

"I figured that the robbers would expect us to think that they would bypass Rawlins, so they'll stop there for sure. Tomorrow or the next day, then lay over a pair of days before they get to Rock Springs. We'll . . ." He hesitated. "I'll be sure and check at Rawlins for any possible sales."

"What hotel are you staying at here?" she asked.

He started to give a name but remembered that he didn't have a hotel room yet. "I guess I don't have one. I went straight to the U.S. marshal's office, left my bag there, and went right to work."

"Then you can at least walk me back to my hotel. It isn't far, but it's dark out and we have to go past several saloons."

At her hotel room door a few minutes later, she lifted her face to be kissed. He let his lips touch hers softly and came away. She had a vulnerable look for a moment; then her expression changed.

"No, Mr. Long, I'm not inviting you into my room again. I'm sure you can rent a room from the clerk downstairs. I'll see you on the train promptly at five-thirty A.M. Good night, Mr. Long."

She turned, pushed open her door, and stepped inside. She closed the door, and a moment later Longarm heard her turn the key in the lock. He lifted his brows in silent recognition. He had lost the first round with Kimberly Walkenhorst, but there would be another round tomorrow.

Marshal Long went downstairs to get a room for the night, then hurried back to the U.S. marshal's office. B.R. sat just inside the reception area waiting for him.

"Boss figured you'd be needing your things. How did your meet go with the cute little lady with the long brown hair?"

"Not productive. I'll be on the five-thirty train in the morning. Thanks for your help here in Laramie and for the Gladstone. You'll hear on the wire when and where we catch this pair. You can be sure that we'll get them, one way or another."

Longarm went back to the hotel for an early bedtime. Tomorrow would be a better day. It just damn well had to be!

Chapter 6

The next morning, Longarm stepped on board the train with five minutes to spare. He checked the two passenger cars, but Kimberly Walkenhorst was not there. He stood with the conductor at the entrance to the first car on the mixed train. Just before the trainman took up the step, Kimberly came running to the car, hair, clothes, and a traveling bag all flying.

As soon as she was settled on the coach car, Kimberly went to sleep. Longarm took his usual run through the two passenger cars, but found no one who looked like an old lady who might be Riane Moseley, the jewel thief.

He went back to the seat beside Kimberly, and soon the train pulled into Rawlins.

Kimberly staggered off the car and to the nearest hotel, the Benedict, where she registered and went to sleep. Longarm took a room next to hers, left his gear there, and had breakfast. The clock showed six-thirty. The jewelry stores wouldn't open until eight.

Rawlins was part of the U.S. marshal's district covering the whole territory of Wyoming, so the deputy marshal didn't have to check in. The sheriff probably wouldn't be awake until noon.

After a leisurely breakfast, Longarm put on his overcoat and walked the town's one main street, all two blocks of it, with businesses on both sides and the train tracks one block over.

He found only three places that sold jewelry, and one of them doubled as a watch and clock repair store.

"Well, old son, looks like you're getting nowhere damn fast. How do we stop this pair?" Longarm asked himself. He had no answers.

He stopped by the sheriff's office and found only one sleepy deputy, who said the sheriff would be in about ten o'clock. Figured.

Longarm helped the owner open the first jewelry store. He leaned against the front door until the proprietor came marching down the street and let him in. After the usual warning about the jewel robbery and the pair trying to sell diamonds, Longarm moved on to the next store.

He finished talking to the other jewelry store owners a half hour later. They would send a runner to the sheriff's office if any strangers came in with diamonds or other precious stones for sale. That meant Longarm would be spending a lot of time at the small local law building.

When Rawlins's one bank opened at ten o'clock, Longarm walked in and talked to the president and owner, M. J. Merriweather. The man knew about the jewel robbery and that the crooks were heading west.

"Yes, I do buy a diamond now and then, as an investment. If the economy goes up and down, it doesn't effect the price of diamonds. We just came out of a small recession, when hard times had settled in. But the price of a good diamond didn't vary more than a couple of dollars either way. Diamonds are forever in the banking business. Wish I had more money invested in them."

"The problem is they don't produce interest," Longarm said. The banker nodded and said if anyone tried to sell him some stones, he'd send a teller running to the sheriff's office.

Longarm dropped in at the hotel. Kimberly's key wasn't in her box at the clerk's desk, so he figured she was still sleeping. Might be a good time to have a talk. He slid out of his heavy overcoat and took off his gloves and carried them as he went up to the second floor. He knocked twice on her door before he heard a response. When the panel opened a crack, he saw a bleary-eyed beauty staring at him.

"Still the middle of the night," she whined. "Go way."

"We need to talk."

"Right now?"

"Sooner the better," Longarm said.

She opened the door a little more, and her frown changed to a smile. "Sure, why not? Come on in."

Kimberly stepped back and let him slip inside, then closed the door and locked it. Longarm turned to take a good look at her. She wore a thin silk nightgown that was almost transparent. He sucked in a quick breath. She was slender, with a flat little stomach and breasts that surged out much more than he had guessed.

She grinned as she watched him.

"You're staring at my nearly naked body," Kimberly said.

"Ayuh. You expected me to ignore you?"

"I hoped that you wouldn't. You're a great surprise to wake up to." She undid the tie in the front of the silk gown and it fell apart from neck to hem. "At least you aren't running away."

"Not one of my bad habits." Longarm took two steps toward her, caught her shoulders, and pulled her to him. He kissed her hard, with a hunger they both could feel. He pressed her big breasts against his jacket as his arms went around her.

When their kiss ended, she looked up at him with a soft smile. "I think it's time, Custis Long. We'll get this first one out of the way and then it'll be easier. No more posturing or pretending. I've wanted you since the first moment I saw you." She took his hand and led him to the bed.

In one motion she threw the covers back from the sheets and sat on the edge of the bed. He settled down beside her.

"I should be at the sheriff's office waiting for some word from the jewelry stores."

"The robbers aren't even be in town yet. This is our day and our night." She kissed him, then took off his jacket. A minute later she unbuttoned his vest and his shirt and her hands rubbed his bare chest.

Longarm pushed her silk nightgown apart, and his hand closed around her breast. He felt the heat of it and could

53

almost see her nipple surge larger and throb with hot blood.

"What a wonderful way to wake up and greet the day," Kimberly said.

He shucked out of his vest and shirt, then pushed her over on the bed and lay half on top of her. He felt her hands at his crotch. Longarm kissed her lips and left her sighing. Then he pushed back the soft silk and spread a ring of kisses around her large breast. He moved from one to the other and at last nibbled on her throbbing nipples until she cried out in delight.

She pushed him away, sat up, and undid his belt and the buttons at his fly. Her hands found his hardness and pulled it out.

"Oh my!" she whispered. "Such a big man!" She bent and kissed the purple tip of him, then worked on his boots and pulled them off, followed by his pants and his long underwear.

"I want you all naked and beautiful," she whispered. She had dropped the nightgown and stood before him bare and with hot, dancing eyes.

She shivered in the chill of the unheated hotel room.

"Under the covers," Longarm instructed. She crawled in beside him, and he pulled the sheet and quilts over them.

"I can see the headline in the local paper now: Out-of-town couple freeze to death while making love."

Kimberly giggled. She caught his erection under the covers and pumped it.

"Easy," he said. She rolled on top of him and kissed him hard; then her mouth was open, and she stabbed her tongue down his throat. Her hips pounded three times against his; then she sighed and tried to relax.

"Easy. We have all day."

"And all night. I want you to screw me until I'll be sore for a week."

Longarm grinned at her, then found her breasts with his hands and caressed them until he heard her breathing higher and heavier.

"Darling Custis, I want to do it some strange way I've never done before."

He kissed her and then nodded. "I have a couple of ideas."

She laughed and reached down and pumped his erection. "I just bet you do. But right now I have you all to myself." She caught one of his hands and pushed it down to her crotch. She rolled off him, and the blankets came between them, and both of them laughed.

When they had the covers straight, she pushed his hand to her crotch.

"Feel me down there! I'm so hot and juicy I'm about to go wild."

His fingers walked around her treasure hole and massaged up her leg, then down, and at last brushed over her wet nether lips.

"Oh, yes!" she crooned and pushed her crotch upward toward his hand. Again he brushed her moist lips, and she purred like a tiger cat. He felt her legs spread apart, and gently he searched for her tiny node, her female penis, and when he found it he rubbed it four times.

"Oh, my god! What's that?"

"You've never played your harp down here?"

"No, nobody ever told me. Do it again."

He strummed the button a dozen times, and before he knew she was so close, she screeched in wonder and her hips pounded against him. Her whole body shook as if she were in an earthquake, and the vibrations drilled through her body, making it bounce and shake like an aspen in a windstorm.

She climaxed five times, then again, and her eyes went so large he could see white all around them.

"Great guns in the morning, but that was fine." She kissed him, then caught his hand and moved it down. "Do it again."

He found her clit, then pushed one finger into her slot as deep as it would go before he twanged the node. Her eyes splayed wide again, and after only four touches of the sensitive organ, she exploded again. He kept his finger inside her, gently stroking in and out as she rattled through another series of climaxes.

She wailed like an alley cat in heat and pounded her hips against him, then at last gave a long sigh and closed her eyes. A few moments later her eyes popped open.

"I forgot about you!" She ducked under the covers, and he could feel her long brown hair on his thighs. Then she found what she wanted and slid his erection into her mouth gently, sucking it and bobbing her head up and down. He threw back the covers to watch her. It wouldn't take long. Longarm let her continue for a moment more, then stopped her.

"What, how? I want you inside me."

He pushed the covers back and positioned her on her hands and knees. She looked back over her shoulder.

"Like this? Oh, from the . . . from the back?"

He spread her knees a little, knelt behind her, and a second later eased into her hot, moist hole. She nearly fell forward. Kimberly brayed softly, turned, and looked at him. "Marvelous. Just the best it's ever been. How do you keep topping it all the time. Oh, God. Oh, God, I think I'm going to come again!"

She did, with a wail and cry that he figured half those on the second floor heard. She trailed off, but kept on her hands and knees.

He stroked into her gently, then harder.

"Screw me good, Custis! Screw me as fast as you can!"

He obliged. Long, searing strokes that heated him faster than usual. He caught the crease where her hips met her torso and used the handholds as he blasted into her as fast and hard as he could. She fell once, but came up quickly.

Again she looked over her shoulder and smiled, and it sent him off into a grunting, surging climax that showered the room with fresh stars and exploded the universe in a big bang. With his final drive against her round bottom, she fell forward on her stomach and slowly extended her legs until he lay on top of her back, still fully inserted.

"Never again will it be so marvelous," Kimberly whispered. Then she took a big breath and rested.

Gradually his gushing breath slowed, and he at last sucked enough air into his lungs to replace the used-up oxygen in his bloodstream. His breathing eased and he closed his eyes. He could go to sleep so easily.

She roused him, moving enough to let him know he should get off. He slid to the sheet beside her and pulled the covers up to cover their still-steam-heated bodies.

She stared at him through half-open eyes.

"That different enough?" he asked.

She pushed over and kissed him, then snuggled against his chest. "Just tremendous, never better."

"Good. Now how are we going to grab those robbers?"

She frowned. "Longarm, shut up and let me enjoy. I love getting . . . getting screwed that way. It was wonderful, and I want to revel in the afterglow for as long as possible. Hold me tight."

He put his arms around her, one hand cupping a breast, his lips kissing her neck.

"Yeah, that's better," she said.

Twenty minutes later, Longarm slid out of bed and dressed. Kimberly had drifted into a quiet sleep. When he was ready to leave, he kissed her awake.

"Again," she said, eyes still closed.

"Soon," he said. "I need to check in with the sheriff and make the rounds. I'll be back."

"Damn right you will," Kimberly said. She smiled and went to sleep.

No one had asked the sheriff to come check on a diamond buyer. Longarm made the circuit, first stopping at the bank to cash a voucher for fifty dollars. The banker had not been approached by anyone to sell a diamond, either a little old lady or an energetic young man.

The jewelry stores had the same message. He told them to be especially watchful the next day, when the robbers would probably be in town.

Back at the hotel, Longarm got hot soup, sandwiches, and two bottles of cold beer from the dining room and took them up to Kimberly's room. He tried the door. She hadn't bothered to lock it.

Kimberly came upright in the bed when he called her name. Her eyes went wide for a moment, and she looked down at her naked breasts and then grinned and held out her arms to him. He sat on the bed and hugged her, kissed her breasts then her lips.

"Lunchtime," he said. Her eyes widened.

"Yes, I'm as hungry as a she-bear who's just been bred. What's to eat?"

After they ate, they bundled up against the cold and walked the street. A light fall of dry snow came down as they went

57

from store to store, just enough to dust the ground and the boardwalk with white. The clouds with the snow brought a little warmer temperature, but Longarm figured it was still near thirty degrees.

He bought Kimberly a colorful scarf in the general store, along with a box of rounds for his .44–40 Colt.

They stopped at each of the jewelry stores again, and each time he edged her away from the diamond rings and back to the street. She told him more about the robbers.

"The woman, Riane, was an actress and something of a playwright as well. She had a play produced in Chicago, but it never did well. No one seems to know when they stopped being actors on the stage and went in for jewels. First they did thievery at parties, going through reticules and purses; then they tried night burglaries in rich folks' houses."

"Then the big mark with the robbery at the ball," Longarm said. "It must have been planned well to do it with only two of them."

"The Chicago police said the whole thing was planned and timed down to the last second. They knew precisely what they were doing and where the guards were and how to take them out. It was a masterpiece of crime."

"Now we need a masterpiece of our own."

They checked in with the last jeweler, the one with clocks as well, and then hurried through the new snow toward their hotel. Longarm's watch showed a little after three in the afternoon.

"Whatever are we going to do the rest of the day, until time for supper?" Kimberly asked as they went into her room.

"I just thought of something," Longarm said.

Five minutes later they had undressed and snuggled under the covers to stay warm. They made love twice more that afternoon and had a big supper in the hotel dining room.

A traveling troupe of actors presented a play at the community hall that night, and Longarm and Kimberly went to see it. Afterward they had coffee and rolls in a cafe.

"Absolutely the worst *Hamlet* I've ever seen," Longarm said.

"I enjoyed it. I'm not a drama snob. Even when they forgot their lines, I didn't mind. Of course that's the first time I've seen *Hamlet* staged." She reached across the table and squeezed his hand. "Are you ready? Let's hurry back to the room. I just thought of something new I want to try."

Longarm chuckled. "Reckon we can leg it over to the hotel. But I'm telling you true blue I don't have the slightest idea what you could be referring to."

Longarm lied. Her idea turned out to be new for her but not so new to him.

Just after midnight a booming explosion rocked their room. Longarm sat up in bed.

"It came from this floor, maybe next door," he said. He pulled on pants and a shirt and ran into the hall barefooted, with his Colt .44–40 in his hand. The hallway was filled with smoke. The door on room 212, next to Kimberly's, had been blown outward and lay in the hall. Smoke gushed from the room.

Longarm dropped low under the smoke and looked inside the room he had rented. The place had been ripped to pieces, the window broken inward, with glass on the floor.

Someone had tried to kill him. Good thing he'd stayed the night with Kimberly. Doors all down the hallway opened and heads poked out. Everyone had a question.

"It's over," Longarm called. "No danger. Go back to bed. A bomb went off in a room. No fire, no danger. Go back to sleep."

He waited a few minutes for the smoke to clear out, then checked his room again. Nothing burned; there was just a mass of smoke from the black powder bomb. They always made a gush of black smoke. At least the bombers could have used dynamite.

He kicked the door and went back into Kimberly's room. He pushed the dresser in front of the window. It covered up most of it. That would cut down the chances of anybody hitting this room with a bomb.

The big question now: Who had tried to kill him?

Chapter 7

With the cold dawn, Longarm awoke, dressed, and examined the damage to his rented quarters. He had moved his baggage into Kimberly's room before the blast, so none of his property had suffered.

He found no evidence of shrapnel damage, so the powder must have been in a sack or some other soft casing. The explosion alone would have killed anyone in the room.

Longarm checked with the clerk downstairs and found he had already been assigned a new room, 227.

"I'll take it," Longarm said. "But keep my record down here as being in 212. That way I won't get any more midnight visits from bombers."

The clerk nodded and changed the notation on his records. The dining room hadn't opened yet. Longarm warmed his hands over the coal stove in the lobby, then backed up to it and turned around and around to warm the cold places. After twenty minutes of roasting, he walked upstairs to Kimberly's unheated room. He watched Kimberly as she slept.

She rolled over, throwing the covers down and exposing her breasts, which surged into view. Longarm grinned. She was some woman, with bigger tits than he had seen in a long time. She seemed to like to make love as much as a man.

Kimberly moved again, making her breasts roll and bounce. Her eyes snapped open.

"Sir, you've been staring at my twin ladies here. Would you like to pet them?"

Longarm laughed. "How long have you been awake?"

"Ever since you came in the room. Slip in here into this nice warm cocoon. We have lots of time for wake-up lovemaking."

"Yesterday you called it screwing."

"That's when I'm hot and horny and wanting you inside me. I need to get really heated up before I can talk sexy."

"About your offer of bed space, you forget I'm working on a case. Now I also need to figure out who's trying to kill me. You do remember the bomb last night that blew my room next door into a smashed-up shambles?"

"A real loud one."

"Besides loud, deadly. Glad the bomber didn't hit this room by mistake."

"What kind of bomb?" Kimberly asked.

"I'd guess black powder. The smoke had the black powder smell."

"Figures. Before he turned to acting, Eric Heinrich was a powder monkey in a coal mine in Pennsylvania. He's good with explosives of all types."

"Glad you told me now."

"You didn't ask. I said I know a lot more about this pair than you do."

"Breakfast?"

She nodded, then dressed, and they went downstairs, risking the hotel food and not the cold weather outside. After they had eaten, Kimberly scurried into the lobby to get warm, and Longarm headed for the general store.

"You sell any black powder yesterday?" he asked. He showed his badge and the store owner nodded.

"That I did, three times as I remember. Twenty pounds to old Harry who's blowing out stumps, ten pounds to a man I didn't know who said he had some rocks to break up. Then I sold two pounds to Charlie White to use to reload his shotgun shells."

"One of the men you didn't know?"

"True, town man, dressed nice. Bought the ten-pound sack and some burning fuse. Said he didn't trust dynamite. Most of my customers want the gelatin sticks now. Easier to work with most times."

"But not so stable. You ever see a box of dynamite explode when it's dropped too hard?"

"Never have, never want to. You need some dynamite?"

"No. Can you describe the stranger who bought the powder?"

"Yep. Inch or so under six feet. I had to look up to him. I hate that. Maybe a hundred and sixty pounds or so, dark hair, and he had a full beard and mustache."

"What did he wear?"

"Town suit and vest, no watch chain."

"You have a good memory. What about the color of his eyes?"

"Don't remember."

Longarm thanked the man. The powder buyer could have been Eric Heinrich. They must be tired of being chased. But that would mean the pair had come in on yesterday's train with time enough to find out Longarm's room number. From now on he'd use a different name when he checked in at hotels.

What next? He made the rounds of the just-opening jewelry stores.

Longarm talked with a large man with a green eyeshade and the softest hands he'd ever seen. The man could pick up a pin in his big mitts and take a delicate watch apart and repair it in the wink of his eye. He was a gentle giant.

"This might be the day," Longarm said to the big man, whose name was Running. "I think they were in town last night, but I'm not sure."

"I send someone to the sheriff's office with a note if I think I have one of them in the office, right?" Running asked.

"Right. We've had no reports of the pair being armed, but I wouldn't doubt that he carries a derringer; perhaps she does as well."

The big man nodded, and a fraction of a second later Longarm stared down the sawed-off muzzles of a double-barreled shotgun.

Running swung the weapon away and it vanished under the counter.

"I get a call now and then to bring this little charmer into play. I usually don't have much trouble with gunmen. Put two in boot hill last year with one round. Blew out a twenty-dollar window at the same time, but it was worth it. Then I found out there was a hundred-dollar reward out on one of the bastards, so I more than broke even."

Longarm smiled. "I'm glad you have a steady trigger finger. Hope we hear from you today."

He continued on the three-store circuit, then went to see Sheriff Gavin Faber, since the bank wasn't open until ten. He hadn't talked to the sheriff yet. These days Faber played the role of town sheriff, not gunman. Longarm had met him before, when his gun often turned hot.

Gavin Faber had arrived in the small railhead town of Rawlins with the first steam engine, and promptly killed two men robbing a gambling hall, and wounded two more the next day who tried to steal the railroad payroll clerk's money bag, with five thousand dollars in it.

The railroad set him up as its town marshal before any real town existed, and he stayed. He'd been elected sheriff every four years ever since. He claimed he'd lived sixty hard years, so now he left most of the outside law work and all the gun action to his two deputies.

Sheriff Gavin Faber grinned and held out his hand. "Longarm, good to meet you again. We had a didey-do couple of years back out in the dry country. Good to see you."

Longarm took the firm grip, returned it, and nodded. "Good to be through here again, Faber. You've heard about my current assignment?"

"Yep. Tough one. Actors! They should stick to the stage. Have trouble enough finding some hombre when we get a good description of him. Now they change their spots on us, their clothes, and their faces. Just ain't fair."

"Makes it harder. Hear about that bomb in my room at the hotel last night? I figure this Heinrich must be in town and sent me a calling card."

63

" 'Pears so. One of my boys made a report on it. Looks like your robber is in town with the woman. Only three jewelry stores hereabouts. Got one of my deputies watching the biggest one from across the street."

"My thanks, Sheriff Faber. We need all the help possible on this one. Not a case I cottoned to from the git go. But here we are."

Longarm stood from the chair where he had sat when he first came in. The lawman stood as well.

"Hope we can corral these two varmints for you here in Rawlins. Not much trouble around here this time of year. Another good snowfall and things will really slow down."

They shook, and Longarm said he'd check in every hour or so and hope they made some contact. He went back to the street, ducking into the fur collar of his overcoat against the sharp wind. It carried small bits of snow. Just a harbinger of coming bad weather from the looks of the black, angry clouds to the west.

Longarm found a small cafe across from the second biggest jewelry store in town and went inside. He sat near the front window and watched the jewelry store for an hour while he warmed himself over two cups of black, hot coffee. He saw only six people go into the jewelry store. None stayed long, and he saw no reaction from the clerk inside.

He gave up and went back to the sheriff's office, but they had had no communication from any of the jewelers. Longarm decided the day would be a long one.

He went to the hotel, and as soon as he came in the door, the clerk waved at him.

"I have a message for you," the clerk said.

He took a folded piece of paper and handed it to Longarm. The deputy marshal opened it and saw that all it said was "Hi! I'm Diane Snook, a correspondent and reporter for the *Chicago Sun* newspaper. When can we get together to talk?" It was signed Diane. No room number or place to contact her. Just as well. He didn't need a bunch of newspaper stories in the Chicago papers about not being able to catch the robbers.

He had started to walk toward the stairs when a young woman came toward him. She made eye contact and smiled.

"You must be U.S. Deputy Marshal Custis Long, the famous Longarm. Hello, I'm Diane Snook." She held out her hand and he took it. Her grip was firm, and her stare never left his face. She was small, slender, and shapely, with blue eyes and shoulder-length red hair.

"Yes, the reporter from Chicago." Longarm shook his head. "I'm sorry, but anything about the case will have to come through official channels. That would be Chief Marshal Ambrose Clapshaw in Laramie. His district covers all of Wyoming Territory."

"I talked to him yesterday," she said, smiling. "Now I want to get the real facts and the lowdown and just what you're doing to catch these two robbers. Chicago is extremely interested in this case, as are most of the state's politicians."

Longarm liked her smile, the sleek way her clothes outlined her delicious body. Breasts not overly large but proportioned to her slender frame, and she wasn't afraid to let the world see them under her tight dress.

"Miss Snook. I understand your position. All I can do is handle my work assignment. It doesn't include talking with the press, especially the Chicago papers, which haven't been at all kind to the Chicago police or the marshal's office."

"Yeah, true. We got on you a little. But that's our job. Any good newspaper has to be a pinprick, to dig into cases like this and look for graft or collusion. Still seems too easy for the robbers the way they got away with so many jewels with police and special guards there."

"I wouldn't know about that, Miss Snook. Now, if you'll excuse me, I do have some more work to do."

"Oh, I understand," she said, flashing him a pretty smile. Her teeth were even, white. "I see you've talked to all of the jewelry store owners. Good move. It makes it a lot harder for the robbers to sell any of their goods. This time you even talked to the banker. Smart. I'll have that all in my story. You see, I have to write about what you're doing whether you talk to me about it or not."

"I understand that. Freedom of the press. It's in the constitution. I also have the freedom to do my job. Talking to you would make my job harder, maybe impossible."

"Oh, I won't write anything you tell me is off the record. I wouldn't do that. I decided that when I started on this trip. Now that I've met you, I'm more convinced that I want to help, not hinder, you."

"Good. The best help is not to use my name, not to write anything at all about what I'm doing."

"Oh, well, I can't go quite that far. I mean, what you do and who you see is a matter of public record, or I see you do it myself. I can use all of that."

Something brushed his sleeve. Longarm looked down and saw Kimberly standing beside him. She wore a dress he'd never seen. Her hair had been brushed, and she'd applied just a touch of rouge to her cheeks and brightener to her lips. She looked good enough to eat, right off a tin plate, sitting around a cold camp fire in a freezing rain.

Diane looked at Kimberly and blinked. "Oh, yes, you must be that partially employed girl detective for the insurance company, Kimberly. I've heard about you. I understand the two of you are sharing a room here at the hotel."

Kimberly swung her hand at Diane, her fingers frozen into a claw with nails unsheathed. Longarm caught Kimberly's arm before any scratching could take place. He pulled Kimberly to one side and looked back at the reporter.

"Like I said, Miss Snook, no comment, no story about any case I'm working on. Interesting meeting you. Good-bye." He caught Kimberly with his arm around her waist and propelled her toward the dining room. Early for lunch, but at least it would get Kimberly away from the reporter.

"That bitch!" Kimberly spat. "I saw how she was looking at you, like she wanted to eat you, clothes and all."

"She's a reporter from Chicago working on the diamond robbery story. I told her I couldn't give her a story. End of conversation with her."

"She's no reporter."

Longarm released his firm grip on her near the dining-room door and turned her toward him. "Just how do you know that she's not a reporter?"

"Because reporters are men, and not that pretty and with that good a figure, and dressed so . . . so . . . so fetching!"

"Fetching?" Longarm chuckled. "If'n I didn't know any better, Miss Walkenhorst, I'd say you were a bit on the jealous side."

"Jealous? Of a witch like that? She's the kind of woman who eats men up for breakfast and spits them out for lunch. Jealous? Of all the silly, ridiculous . . ." She stopped and took a big breath, then faced him. "Yeah, a little jealous. Come on, Cowboy, let's have an early lunch."

They settled for soup and bread sticks and three cups of coffee.

"How did she find you?" Kimberly asked.

"Who?"

"The girl, the reporter."

"Oh, her. She had the room clerk point me out as I checked my box for messages."

"Hussy. I bet she doesn't even use underwear."

"Just doing her job. You should be sympathetic. She's doing a man's job, like you are. Don't you have a little womanly sympathy for her?"

"Not an ounce. What did she say to you?"

"She asked me for an interview about the robbery case, what progress I was making on it."

"So you told her?"

"No, I just said I didn't tell her a thing. Any statement would have to come from the U.S. marshal's office. While we're in the Territory of Wyoming, that would be from Laramie." Longarm frowned at his pretty dinner companion. "Now please be quiet and let me finish my lunch. This is good clam chowder soup. I wonder where they got the clams."

"I still don't trust her."

"Feminine intuition?"

"Whatever you call it, she's trouble." Kimberly looked at Longarm with a small frown. Her voice dropped to a whisper. "I thought . . . I thought that I was taking care of your needs pretty good."

Longarm watched her a moment, then grinned. His voice was also low so no one else could hear. "Hell, lady, if you took care of me any better up there in your bed, I'd be so worn out I couldn't walk. Now don't worry about that woman. I'll probably never see her again."

"I hope not."

"You through with your lunch?" Longarm asked. "Time we check in with the sheriff. You should meet this man. He's one of the old-time real Western lawmen, who has done his share of gunwork against some of the worst outlaws on the prairie."

A few minutes later they stepped out of the hotel into a full-blown snowfall. It came down like fluttering rain, and already the street and boardwalk were covered with a beautiful white blanket.

Chapter 8

The second day in Rawlins produced no attempt by the robbers to sell any diamonds. Not even the sniff of an attempt. Longarm changed rooms at the hotel for the night, and no one attacked them. He and Kimberly left the next morning on the mixed train, heading for Rock Springs. It got out of Rawlins at seven-thirty, after a short layover for a repair on a wheel bearing.

The snow that had started the day before had piled up to more than a foot but had not slowed the trains. They bolted snowplow blades on the front of the engines, and they splattered and scattered the moderate snowfall. The blades could remove a foot or more of snow from the tracks if it wasn't the wet, icy kind.

Longarm and Kimberly arrived in Rock Springs shortly before ten A.M., after only a minor delay, and found that "the Springs" as the rail men called it, had more snow, almost two feet on the level, with a lot of windblown drifts.

A special engine and snowplow would precede the train as it headed out of the 6,271-foot-high Rock Springs, toward the Utah border another sixty miles away.

Longarm and Kimberly hoofed it to the closest hotel. The boardwalks had been scooped, some to make a three-foot-wide pathway, some the entire width of the walk, and the snow pushed into the street, where the horses and wagons smashed it into a dirty mush.

The weather had turned cold, and Longarm figured it was near zero as they unbundled from their overcoats and mittens and tried to get their fingers warm enough to sign the hotel register. They had talked about using false names, and both took separate rooms, she as Mary Jones and he as Will Black.

Kimberly unpacked and retreated to the lobby and the pair of big coal stoves that the clerk kept burning hot. Longarm put on his overcoat and mittens and braved the cold weather. He walked to the county building and checked with the sheriff, then found the four stores in town that sold diamonds and other gems. Two of them were also watch-repair stores.

The second jeweler snorted when Longarm started with his story.

"I'd say you're about twenty minutes too late. I bought two diamonds this morning from a middle-aged woman on the fat side who wore heavy glasses. Said she had to get back to Omaha for her mother's funeral. Didn't know her, but the diamonds were beauties and I got them for about sixty percent of value. Better than I can do wholesale."

Longarm looked at the two gems. One a two-carat and the other a one-carat diamond, blue white and flawless.

"These probably are stolen gems," Longarm said.

The jeweler lost some of his bravado.

"Probably, but you can't prove it?"

"True. We want the seller. If she comes back with another diamond, or if a man stops by, about thirty-five or older, you stall them and get word to the sheriff."

Longarm hurried to the next jewelry store, Rock Springs Jewelry. As he came toward it, he saw a woman on the fat side waddle out of the store. She saw Longarm, turned, and hurried away. Longarm ran toward her. She ducked into the first store on the street, a women's wear shop. Longarm came through the front door with his six-gun out. A woman screamed. Another stared in open-mouthed amazement, lifted her hands and dropped a dress a seamstress was working on, exposing her breasts.

"Sorry, ladies. A woman just came in here. Where did she go?"

"She charged in and ran through the door into the back," said a woman who seemed to be in charge. "I never seen her before. I yelled at her, but she kept running. Kind of on the fat side."

"Thanks. I'm a lawman." He hurried to the door, pushed it open, and stood to one side. A handgun fired from the back, and the round whistled through the opening and hit the door frame in front. One of the women in the store fainted.

Longarm dove through the opening, hit on his shoulder, and rolled behind some boxes. He heard a door bang at the back of the forty-foot storage area. He came to his feet running and sprinted to the door. He squatted beside it and pushed it open. He saw a woman near the back door of another store. She fired, but before he could return the hot lead, she ducked through the door.

Longarm rushed across the sixty feet to the store and opened the door. This time there was no gunfire.

He stepped inside and listened.

He heard nothing.

It was the back room of a hardware store. There were stacks of horse collars, piles of boxes filled with goods, rows and alleys and dozens of hidey-holes where the woman could be lurking. He began checking them, with his Colt at the ready. A man came into the back room, picked up an item he needed, and went back to the front.

After fifteen minutes, Longarm began to wonder what had happened to the woman. She had to be here somewhere. He stopped. Had he heard something? He strained, listening. Then it came, the soft closing of the door into the front of the store.

Longarm ran that way, checking both sides as he went. He saw no one. He lifted the latch quietly and pulled the door open.

He could see half the store. Nowhere did he find the fat woman. One lady customer stood ten feet away checking some cooking pots. A salesman waited beside her.

Longarm hurried toward them.

"I'm U.S. Deputy Marshal Custis Long. A woman just came out of your back room over there. Which way did she go?"

The clerk frowned. "Sorry, I didn't see anyone leave the storage room. Nobody's allowed back there."

"She ran in from the alley. I've been chasing her. You must

71

have seen her. About five-three and chunky, fat really. Didn't you see her?"

The clerk and the customer shook their heads. "I'm afraid I've been looking at these pots," the customer said. She stood well over five-foot-five and was slender, in her forties. She couldn't possibly be Riane Moseley.

Longarm searched the rest of the store. There was no woman in the place. The back door! She had pulled that old trick on him. He rushed past the surprised clerk and into the storage room. Just inside the rear door he found what he'd feared he would—the brown coat the woman had worn and beside it the wrappings of a bedspread that would make a slender woman appear to be fat.

He stepped into the alley and saw a woman's boot marks leading away from the door. They showed plainly in the snow, then were mashed into oblivion by the passage of a wagon through the alley.

Longarm slammed his hand against a cardboard box and showered snow off its top. He'd almost had her, again. How could she be so slippery?

He talked to the owner of the jewelry store he had seen her leaving. The man said he'd bought one diamond. She had offered him six. He chose one and paid about half of its value. Longarm warned him what to do if she came in again.

He checked and found out the woman hadn't been to the other jewelry stores. He gave them the warning and the penalties and urged them to contact the sheriff if they saw either of the pair trying to sell diamonds.

Longarm went back to the sheriff. Clive Anderson knew about the diamond robbery. He was sympathetic but had only three deputies, and one of them was on night duty.

"What I want to do is check all passengers loading onto the outgoing trains, east or west. One each way this afternoon, right?"

"Right, but how do we check them?" Sheriff Anderson asked.

"We're looking for a woman five-three and a man five-ten. Everyone else we pass through automatically. Those people who fit that description, I want to talk to. These two I'm hunting are actors and use makeup and costumes to change their appearance.

72

They can't change their eye color or height. Her eyes are blue and his are brown. This is the only way I can figure out to stop them."

The sheriff agreed. He posted his two deputies at the train that was due to leave at two-thirty, going east. The deputies found three short women, whom Longarm checked. One was Indian, one a Mexican, and the other truly a fat woman. None could be Riane Moseley. Only two men answered the height description. One, a cowboy and no hiding it. The other one, a drummer with a full set of goods, heading for home.

Longarm had coffee at the sheriff's office and worried about it. The afternoon train was due out westbound about five. The sheriff worked one passenger-car entrance and Longarm the other one. The marshal checked twenty-four people who stepped up to the coach. Only one came anywhere near being five-three and female, a pregnant woman with brown eyes, and no chance she could be faking her condition. Longarm talked to the sheriff, who'd seen one man who looked good for a while, but he turned out to be a Catholic priest with soft blue eyes and almost no hair.

Longarm and the sheriff had a beer in a saloon and talked it over.

"I don't think they got out of town," Sheriff Anderson said. "They didn't get on the train unless they rode the rails. Not a chance they can drive a rig out of here and make it to Salt Lake City. Roads won't be open for a week."

"So where are they?"

"Hotel?"

"Probably," Longarm said. "If I was holing up for a couple of days, I'd have my meals sent in. Which hotel will take meals up to the rooms?"

"Both of them. Costs double."

"Worth a check." Longarm pulled on his overcoat and gloves and crunched his way through the snow on the boardwalk down to his hotel. Kimberly read a magazine in the lobby near the big stove. She saw him come in. He waved, gave her his overcoat, and went to talk to the cashier at the dining room.

"Yes, we have several people who order meals in their rooms," the older woman said.

"How do they order?"

"Usually someone comes down and tells me what they want. I send it up with a boy, and he collects the cost of the meal and brings it to me."

"Has a woman about five-three been ordering meals?"

"A dark-haired woman?"

"She changes her hair coloring and could use a wig. It could be any color. What room?"

"Oh, I can't tell you that."

"Yes you can," Longarm said. He produced his badge and identification, and the woman gulped.

"She done something bad?"

"Something, yes, if this is the right one."

"Room 112, first floor, end of the hall, across the lobby."

Longarm left the dining room, loosened the Colt in his cross-draw rig, and marched down the hall to the end. Room 112. He drew the weapon and held it at his side, then knocked on the door.

He heard movement inside, then a muffled voice.

"Yes, who is it?"

He answered, holding his hand over his mouth to confuse what he said.

The woman's voice asked him to repeat it. He did, with much the same sound. The door was unlocked and edged inward.

"Telegram for Riane Moseley," Longarm said, pushing the door inward a foot. A mistake. A dark, short woman stared back at him.

"Riane Moseley?" Longarm asked.

"No, sir, you must have the wrong room," the woman said with a clipped British accent. He saw a man in the back, sitting on the bed. He looked foreign and had the same dark coloring as the woman.

"Sorry," Longarm said and turned and walked away. They were Indians, from India over by China. He marched back to the cashier behind the counter in the dining room. There he asked about any other short women or five-foot-ten-inch men who had been ordering meals in their rooms.

She had one more woman for him, an older lady, in her sixties, the cashier decided. Room 310. Longarm's pulse beat faster.

"You sure she was old, or maybe it was a younger person pretending to be old?"

"No, this one even walked like sixty, a little hitch and a hint of a limp. Moved slowly as if she needed a cane but was too proud to use one."

Longarm nodded and left for room 310, on the top floor. Why would an old woman take a room on the third floor? At the door, he knocked sharply. No response. He waited for twenty seconds, then knocked again. He could hear no movement inside the room.

The marshal turned the doorknob. Locked. He took out his room key and tried it. It fit the keyhole and twisted, but didn't open the lock. Longarm took a stiff wire tool from his pocket. He had used pliers to bend a pair of projections on it to resemble a door key. He inserted it in the lock and turned the wire.

He felt it hit resistance, and he used the bent portion on the handle end to turn it harder. The lock clicked open. He pulled the device out of the door as he heard someone coming up the stairs.

Longarm moved down from 310 to the end of the hall, checking room numbers. A short man in a cowboy hat topped the stairs, went to room 312, opened the door, and vanished inside.

Longarm went back to room 310 and turned the knob. He eased the door inward and surveyed the room in one quick glance. Two people lived there, a man and a woman. Their clothes were scattered around. No one in the room, but they could come back at any moment.

He had just committed an illegal break-in and now was doing an illegal search. He shrugged. Sometimes the law had to be bent a little to catch the owlhoots.

Longarm didn't see any obvious ties to the jewel robbers. No trunk of costumes, no makeup table or small satchel filled with diamonds. He heard someone else on the stairs. He hurried out, closed the door, locked it with his wire key, and walked toward the steps.

An older woman in her sixties paused at the third floor. "Next time I'm getting a ground-level room, even if I have to pay double," she said to the banister. She took another big breath, walked past Longarm without looking at him, and unlocked the door to a room near the end of the hall. Not a chance. That one was obviously a truly old woman.

He wanted to go back in room 310 and search it thoroughly, but he couldn't risk it. What he needed was a lookout on the stairs, halfway up, who could detain anyone for ten minutes and then give a warning if need be. Kimberly could do the job. He headed down the steps. She would be in the room or beside the red-hot coal heater in the lobby.

She wasn't in either spot. He asked the room clerk, who he was sure had an eye for a pretty girl.

"Yes, I did see her go out about a half hour ago. All bundled up, but I'm sure she's the one. She asked me where she could find a woman's clothes shop. I told her just down the street half a block. Miss Flossie's Fashions, the owner calls it."

Longarm thanked the man, collected his overcoat and gloves, and headed toward the front door.

Outside the cold hit him like an icy bucket of water thrown in his face. The temperature had dropped another dozen degrees he was sure. It must be well below zero. The snow crunched under his feet as he walked the partly scooped boardwalk in the direction of the dress shop.

As he came toward it, he saw half a dozen people gathered outside. The lanky form of the sheriff marched up, and the people parted for him. Longarm hurried so he arrived just after the sheriff.

Sheriff Anderson went inside, and Longarm pushed in behind him.

The sheriff looked at a woman who dried her eyes. An occasional sob slipped out.

"Millie, what happened here?"

"Sheriff, it was that awful Nate Varner. He came in and swept her up and called her Bernice and carried her right out the door before I could do a thing. I saw him put her in that sleigh of his, and he went racing down the street. You know how fast that sleigh of his can move."

"Yes, Millie, I know. Now, who was the girl?"

"I don't know. Never saw her before. She wore a red stocking cap and a light blue coat. Pretty little thing. Maybe twenty-five or twenty-six."

"But not a local woman?"

"No, never saw her before today. A stranger."

Longarm spoke up then, a cold fury gripping him. "You said the woman had on a red stocking cap. Did it have a tassel with a white ball on the end of it?"

"Why, yes. Do you know who the girl was?"

Sheriff Anderson looked at Longarm. "Friend of yours?"

"Might be, Sheriff. Where would he have taken her?"

The sheriff motioned Longarm outside. They buttoned up their overcoats and slid into gloves to brave the cold.

"This man Nate Varner is something of a local problem. His wife died a year ago, and he can't accept it. He often comes into town and spots somebody who reminds him of Bernice. He grabs her, puts her in his buggy, or in this case his sleigh, and charges to his cattle ranch five miles outside of town on the River Road. Never known him to hurt any of the women. I've been out there four times in the last six months.

"Usually the women play along with him until somebody comes after them. He doesn't try to hide anything. To him that's Bernice, his wife, and he's just taking her home."

"When do we ride?" Longarm asked, his voice low and hard.

Sheriff Anderson looked up quickly. "Now, no problem here. He ain't never hurt a single one of these women. He won't bother your friend. You can come, but I'm in charge, this is my county, agreed?"

Longarm studied the county sheriff. He didn't know the lawman from Abraham Lincoln, but he'd have to trust him. At last he nodded.

It was nearing full dark when they mounted and rode out the River Road, which ranged to the north and west. The sheriff had provided Longarm with a horse, but no rifle in the scabbard.

The snow in the street was mashed down, but once they left the town, it had been cut by only a wagon or two and half a dozen horses. It leveled out at two feet, but in places had drifted into four-foot walls.

They picked their way around the deep spots and made good time. Five minutes after they left Rock Springs, it began to snow. The flakes came down in a gentle fall, with no wind pushing it.

Longarm had always liked the white fluff, but right now he'd have preferred watching it out his hotel window with a nice warm fire in a fireplace. Except his room didn't have a fireplace.

There were four of them in the posse. Four-to-one odds had always seemed about right to Longarm. No man wanted to take on four guns spitting death-dealing lead.

Three miles out, they angled off the River Road and up a wide valley. A full moon came out. The snow made it easy to see. The river might have been there one day, but now it was only a dry wash. It led into the badlands and on into the Great Divide Basin. The basin was a sink in the middle of the Rocky Mountains, where they opened up and the Continental Divide split, making a circle where all drainage was into the center of the sink. It measured forty-five miles north and south and ninety miles east to west. It looked more like a desert than the middle of Arizona.

Even this flat land fifteen miles from the sink was marginal for grazing range cattle. The posse angled up the wash and over a small hill, and could see lights in a ranch latch-up a mile away.

"We riding right up to the front?" Longarm asked.

"Best way with Nate. He'll think we're neighbors come to pay him a visit. Never known Nate to give us any trouble. Deep down he knows whoever he grabbed isn't his Bernice. It filters through to him, especially if the woman screams and yells at him. Bernice was usually so quiet you lost her."

They rode another half mile and came up less than fifty yards from the ranch house.

Longarm and the sheriff rode in front, and the two deputies behind.

"See," Sheriff Anderson said. "Told you that Nate wouldn't give us any trouble." They rode up another ten yards.

"Hey, Nate, Sheriff Anderson out here," he bellowed. Just then a rifle blasted from a dark doorway in the house, and hot lead sizzled over their heads.

Chapter 9

The rifle shot from Nate Varner's ranch house scattered the four riders. All bailed off their mounts and stood behind them for cover. There was no place else safe from the rifleman in the first-floor window of the modest-size house. The new white snow made the riders easy targets.

"What'n hell?" Sheriff Anderson bellowed. "Nate, you son-of-a-bitch crazy man. Why you shooting at us?"

"You come to take my wife away from me, way you did the other times. She's mine, damn you! She's my Bernice, and ain't a whole passel of you gonna take her back."

"Let's talk about it, Nate. Hell, it's cold and dark out here, and we been on a long ride. You got any of that Tennessee sippin' whiskey left?"

"Got me some. You don't get none. You tricked me last time. You just turn around and ride back to town. This ain't none of your business no account."

"Then let's talk, Nate. You know me. I won't trick you. Hell, I just want what's best for the two of you."

Another rifle round sang over their heads, and the men ducked lower behind their mounts.

"Don't sound like he's in much of a palavering mood," Longarm said.

" 'Deed it don't."

"You keep talking. I'll ride around back and try to get inside," Longarm said.

He put one foot in the left stirrup, grabbed the saddle horn, and threw his right leg over the top of the saddle, hanging on the side of the horse the way the Indian warriors could do. He rode the horse like that to the side, toward the barn about fifty yards away. In the moonlight, Longarm figured the man inside couldn't see his leg showing over the saddle.

Sheriff Anderson yelled again, to try to keep Nate talking.

"Come on, Nate. Getting damn cold out here. I could do with a nip of that good corn you keep for special occasions."

"Ain't no special time for you, Sheriff. Just clear out and leave us alone."

"Can't, Nate. You know that. You don't come out peaceful, means me and the boys got to come in and get you. You did a bad thing again, Nate. Not blaming you. Understand. Won't be nothing against you if'n you give us back the lady. What you done ain't right, Nate. You know that. She just ain't Bernice, and we both understand that."

"Go back to town, Sheriff."

"Nate, think a minute. Would Bernice want you to be doing this? You know that ain't Bernice you got in there. Truth be known, you're positive it ain't Bernice. Right, Nate?"

As the sheriff talked, Longarm urged his mount to walk to the side, and in another ten yards they made it to the back of the barn and there hadn't been any new shots. He was screened from the house now.

The snow had been blown off most of the barnyard and was little more than six inches deep most spots. Behind the barn the wind had been stopped and the snow had drifted in, four feet deep. Longarm swung up on the horse, rode out twenty yards to the foot-high drifts, and worked around the barn.

He rode on to the well house and then to the corral and turned in when he was well behind the house.

Longarm heard the sheriff talking. That meant that Nate must still be at the back window, facing the barn. Longarm bent low and kicked the mount into a rush through the foot-deep snow, toward the side of the house. There was only one window on this side of the building, and he could see no lamplight coming through it. Longarm hoped he wouldn't hear glass breaking or a shotgun sounding off.

He made it to the back wall of the house and dismounted. He pushed back his heavy coat and pulled out his Colt Model T .44-40. It carried five loads.

Longarm lifted up and looked in the side window. It was dark inside, but enough light came through an open door to see that it was a bedroom. The window was nailed in place. He moved to the front of the house and the door most ranchers seldom used. He tried the knob and it turned. Gently he nudged the door open. The door hinges squeaked, but at the same time he heard Nate in the front of the house screeching at the sheriff.

The deputy U.S. marshal edged inside the parlor. Some light came into the area from the door across the room. He could see a living room. Longarm walked across the floor, sliding his steps so he made no sound. At the open door, he looked into the living room. Two lamps burned on a table. On the far side of the room a window faced the barn. Near it stood a man in range clothes, wearing a battered hat.

"Ain't no never mind of yourn what I do with Bernice, Sheriff. Man's home is his castle. Get the hell off my ranch."

Longarm couldn't make out the words the sheriff used, but there was a long reply.

To the side, Longarm could see a couch. On the far end of it sat Kimberly. Her hands were tied in front of her and a cloth gag was bound across her mouth. He waved, and she saw him, and her eyes went wide.

Nate Varner put the rifle down, standing it against the window frame. He shook his head in what must have been frustration.

Longarm lifted his Colt and aimed it at the rancher. When he cocked it, the clicking sound behind him made Varner freeze.

"Don't move, Nate, or it'll be the last thing you ever do in this life. Just turn around slow and easy."

Nate turned until he could see Longarm; then he hurled himself toward Kimberly on the sofa eight feet away. Longarm tracked him, concentrated on his thighs, and fired. The .44 round exploding in the room sounded like a dozen sticks of dynamite going off at once.

Kimberly tried to cry out, but the gag stopped her. Longarm shook his head to rid his ears of the ringing. The round jolted into Nate's left thigh and slammed him onto the wooden floor. He grabbed at his wound and screamed at Longarm.

He saw the man had no handgun. He patted him down. He had no hideout. Longarm went to the window and called for the sheriff to come in.

The U.S. deputy marshal untied the kerchief from around Kimberly's head, and she bleated in anger and fear, then cried. He held her in his arms as she sobbed. The sheriff came in and nudged Nate.

"Nate, looks like you'll live," the sheriff said.

Longarm untied Kimberly's wrists, and she wiped away the tears and took the kerchief. She knelt beside Varner and checked his wounded leg.

"Nate, the bullet didn't come out, so it's going to hurt. You just take it easy, and we'll get you to a doctor who can help you. It's all over, Nate. I'm really not Bernice. You know that now, don't you? I'll get this tied up so you don't bleed anymore."

The sheriff stared at the little scene. "Yep, that's our Nate. He has a hell of a way with the women."

Longarm tore up a tablecloth to make a better bandage and tied up the leg securely for the trip into town. Nate rode one of his horses and didn't talk to anyone.

It took them two hours fighting through the snow in the dark to ride to town. The snow that had fallen on their ride to the ranch had left two inches of new powder and turned the town pure white.

Longarm and Kimberly left their horses with the sheriff and hurried into the hotel. They stood in front of the coal heating stove, turning slowly to warm themselves.

"What will happen to Nate?" Kimberly asked.

"The doctor will cut out the bullet; he'll stay overnight in jail and in the morning be free to ride back to his place. You haven't talked much about being kidnapped."

She watched him a moment and nodded. "I know. He didn't hurt me. He was kind and thoughtful. He didn't even tie me up until he saw you men coming in the moonlight. Nate is still disturbed about his wife dying. At first I told him my name, but he kept calling me Bernice. Poor man. I felt so sorry for him. He won't get in trouble, will he?"

Longarm told her about his history and assured her that the sheriff wouldn't press charges. He turned again, warming his hands.

"How would you like to help me commit a felony?" Longarm asked Kimberly.

"Rape, plunder, pillage, or just a murder?" she asked with a grin.

"Mostly breaking and entering, the judge would call it. I want to see what else I can find in room 310."

He'd told her about the "eat in the room" idea he had, and how he had a good suspect.

"Big trouble is we have to wait until both of them are out."

"Which they wouldn't be about dinnertime if they're eating in."

"True. Then how about some supper for us?"

They ate in the dining room, close to the cashier, but even though Longarm watched carefully, he saw no short woman or fairly tall man order dinners to be taken upstairs.

On the way out, he talked to the same cashier he had spoken to that afternoon. She said nothing had been taken up to room 310 since noon.

Longarm spent two hours in the end of the hall on the third floor freezing his fingernails off. At ten o'clock he went back to the lobby, where Kimberly had settled down with a book, planting her booted feet near the hot coal heater.

"Nothing?" she asked.

"Nothing. Think they'd be hungry by now. Maybe they went out."

"A two-hour supper in this town?"

"Not likely. Maybe they checked out." Longarm paced over to the room clerk. Kimberly watched as he talked with the man. When he came back, his face was puzzled.

"They didn't check out. Paid for two nights in advance. Tonight is the second one. Must be moving on tomorrow."

"Where?"

"Best bet would be the spur line that runs down to Salt Lake

City from the main tracks."

"In the morning?" Kimberly asked.

"Best time to catch a train is when it's running. I'll ask the clerk."

The train left town at twelve-thirty, just after noon.

"I thought you checked a westbound today at four-thirty," Kimberly said.

"True, but they had a long delay up the line due to a landslide. Regular run is twelve-thirty."

No one else had stayed with the fire. Longarm and Kimberley huddled close to it, then decided to go up to their rooms. On Longarm's door was a note tacked with a straight pin. He took it down and read the message.

"Longarm. Need to talk to you. Urgent. I may have an idea about where the jewel thieves are right now. It's nearly ten o'clock P.M. Come to room 110." It was signed Diane Snook.

He showed it to Kimberly, who read it and snorted.

"Isn't that the fancy woman pretending to be a reporter? She's just using this as a ploy to get you in her clutches. I tell you I don't trust that woman."

"If it has something to do with the case, you know I have to go see her."

"If she's naked, don't stay. She's about as much of a reporter as you are."

"Then what's she doing way out here, following the jewel robbers?"

"I don't know and I don't care. I'm going to bed. I hope you're back in five minutes to help me keep warm. I could use a steaming, sexy warming up about now."

He unlocked the door and lit the lamp inside Kimberly's room. She walked in, hugging herself to keep warm.

"Like an icehouse in here," she said. "Please hurry back and keep me warm."

Longarm grinned at the thought and went out the door and down the steps to room 110 on the ground level. When he found it, he could see light coming under the door. Two sharp raps brought sounds from inside.

He had no idea what to expect, so he would be ready for anything. If she knew something about the robber pair, it could be just the bit of information he could use to trip them up. The door swung open.

A barefoot Diane Snook stood there in a dressing gown with the bed behind her rumpled and used.

"Oh, I'm sorry. I disturbed your sleep."

"I wasn't sleeping, just trying to stay warm," she said. "Please come in."

He remembered her: pretty face and sharp features, short, slender, with deep blue eyes and shoulder-length red hair that looked as if it had just been brushed a thousand times.

Longarm stepped into the room, and she closed the door. "Excuse me, but I'm freezing. We can talk just as well with me in bed." She stood by the bed directly in front of him and undid the tie on the robe and slipped it off. Under it she wore only a short nightgown that barely covered her crotch. Through the thin fabric he could see her breasts and swollen pink nipples. As she slid into bed, the cloth slipped up, showing a swatch of brown hair at her crotch.

She didn't seem to notice. She pulled the covers up to her chin and looked at him.

"Yes, ever so much warmer. Now about the robbers. I know for a fact that they're moving out tomorrow on the train at noon, if it gets through the snow. You said they wore disguises. I don't know about that, but I heard a couple talking about Salt Lake City. I heard them say they could probably sell fifteen or twenty diamonds there."

"How do you know this, Miss Snook?

"I told you, I heard a couple talking in the dining room. I sat behind a partition with some plants on it. They thought they were alone. I never got a good look at them until they left and then not at their faces.

"She stands about my height and has dark hair. He's taller, nearly six feet, I'd say, and has lots of brown hair. Both dressed nicely, with a hint of the east. I'm almost sure they were the robbers. I didn't have nerve enough to run up and talk to them."

She snuggled deeper into the covers. "My yes, now it's getting a lot warmer in here. I know it's cold out there. You can join me if you want to. Oh, just to keep warm, of course."

Longarm grinned. "Of course. Don't think I'll be here long enough to get cold. I thank you for your information. I had figured that they would stop in Salt Lake City, but thanks for the confirmation. The train tomorrow, right? I'd decided to move on as well. I would guess you'll be heading in that direction?"

"A girl has to go with the story." She hesitated, watching him with smoldering eyes. "You positive you don't want to slip in here and keep warm for a while?"

"Thanks, but I don't think so. The offer is greatly appreciated. Sort of reminds me of hearing a train whistle. Sometimes it's good to hear, even though you know that you're not going anywhere." He smiled and walked to the door. As his hand turned the knob, she spoke again.

"Oh, Custis."

He looked back. She was on her knees on the bed, the covers dropped and the thin nightgown dangling from one hand, showing off her firm young breasts with wide pink areolas and perky nipples, a slender waist, flat tummy, and the delightful muff at her crotch.

"Just wanted to let you see what you're passing up," she said with a smile. "Maybe next time."

Longarm laughed softly. "Yes, Miss Snook, maybe next time." He went out the door and closed it softly, then hurried down the hall to the lobby. For just a moment, he warmed his hands over the stove; then he marched up the steps and to Kimberly's room on the second floor.

It was always nice to have a choice, but tonight he wanted to be sure and safe and do some thinking. Miss Snook would not have wanted that. He tried the door, unlocked. He stepped inside. The light glowed from the lamp. Kimberly lay on the bed covered with blankets up to her chin.

"About time you got back," she said. "I had serious thoughts of starting without you."

"Be glad to contribute what I can to keeping you warm all night long," Longarm said. He locked the door, pushed the back of the wooden chair under the knob, and sat on the edge of the bed.

"You want some help undressing?" Kimberly asked.

"Help is always good," Longarm said.

86

Kimberly jumped from the bed. She stood before him as naked as Miss Snook had been and for a moment he compared them. Kimberly had bigger breasts, a smaller waist, better sculptured legs, and a far prettier face.

They undressed him in record time, and Longarm kept her warm for two hours before they finally slipped off to sleep.

The next morning, Longarm pulled on his long underwear, two wool shirts and a sweater, then wool pants and two pair of socks. He was still cold. He roused Kimberly, then tied his boot laces and slipped into a heavy jacket.

"As soon as you get dressed, we can go down and warm up by the fire before breakfast," Longarm said.

"Done," she chirped. "But I also need to comb my hair and wash my face and brush my teeth. Ten minutes."

"I'll be back up after you. No, I'll meet you at the stove. Looks like we had more snow last night. I'll check to be sure the train can get through."

Kimberly stopped him before he reached the door.

"Custis, that fancy lady in room 110. Did she try to seduce you last night?"

"Yes, but your try worked much better. Now, get ready. I'm starving for some breakfast."

Chapter 10

The mainliner pulled out of Rock Springs two hours late due to the snowfall. It bulled its way down the tracks across southwestern Wyoming and into northern Utah. A snowplow engine led the way half the time. They fell farther and farther behind their schedule. Twelve hours after leaving Rock Springs, they came to the spur line that went south to Salt Lake City.

They made a quick transfer. Longarm gave up watching for the robbers. He had had no luck before, so he probably wouldn't now. He would rely on trapping them at a diamond sale. That meant he would have to talk to the jewelers as soon as he hit town.

An hour after midnight, they had transferred to the spur line heading to Salt Lake City. The train nudged the last of the new snow off the track and came to a stop in the Salt Lake City depot at four-fifteen A.M.

Longarm woke up Kimberly, and they took a hack to a hotel Longarm remembered, where they registered. Four heavy comforters helped shut out the cold of the unheated rooms.

The U.S. deputy marshal knew he had to be up at seven so he could be ready to talk to the jewelers as soon as they opened. The room clerk showed him a list of stores in town, and he found seven that sold jewelry.

He had a quick breakfast and charged into the icy cold to find the first store. As usual his credentials and badge impressed the store owners, and they agreed to cooperate. They would send someone running to the sheriff's office if they talked to anyone who had diamonds to sell and could be the robbers.

At the fourth store, Longarm chuckled as he saw a familiar face. Diane Snook, the girl reporter, hovered near the store's coal-burning heater and grinned at him.

"Well, stranger, you finally got here. I guessed this would be the first store you'd come to."

"Close. The fourth. What are you doing here, selling your family diamonds?"

"I only wish. We got no diamonds. I'm just a working girl trying to earn a living. Now, you can't deny me the right to follow you around and report on your progress. That's the great American way of journalism."

Longarm didn't want to fight that battle. He shrugged and went to talk to the jewelry store owner. The man said he did buy a diamond now and then, and he would certainly be on the lookout for strangers or travelers selling gems.

Longarm let the girl reporter trail after him as he talked to the next three jewelry store owners. When they left the last store, she slipped on some snow and caught his arm. He put his mittened hand over hers and kept it there.

"Can't have you falling down in the middle of Salt Lake City," he said.

"I'm cold. Could we get a cup of coffee?" she asked.

They found a small restaurant that served coffee and ordered. Many of the eateries didn't offer coffee, since the Mormons frowned on all such strong drink as coffee and tea, as well as beer, wine, and hard liquor.

They held the heavy mugs, warming their hands, and soon had a second cup.

"So, are you getting lots of fascinating material for your articles about the chase of the robbers?"

"No. You won't tell me anything." She said it in a peevish tone, but he saw the smile that simmered under the words.

"How do you send your stories to the newspaper?"

"By telegraph, collect of course. It's easy. I just write it and give it to the key man and he sends it."

"Not exciting at all."

"No, but it is a way to make a living since I have no husband to take care of me and provide for my needs."

"You must have had some chances."

"Yes, one or two." She looked up, smiling her best. "Now, what's next on your busy work schedule?"

"Check with the sheriff's office every hour."

They found the lawman and told him the story. He knew most of it and promised to cooperate. Then they were out on the cold street again kicking snow off the sidewalks.

"Oh, I forgot something at my room. Can I talk you into walking me down two blocks to my hotel?"

Longarm watched her closely, but she seemed to have no other motive.

"I have a scarf that keeps me ever so much warmer. Then I want to follow you to the stores and back to the sheriff's office. I'd love to be there when you catch one of the robbers trying to sell a diamond."

Longarm nodded, and soon they were at her hotel room door. She unlocked the door and invited him in. When he was inside, she slid out of her mittens and heavy coat and turned to him. The dress was tight and the top buttons open to show a hint of cleavage.

"Just want to thank you properly for helping me on my stories," she said.

He took a step backward.

"Oh, is the big strong U.S. deputy marshal afraid of one little girl reporter?"

"Not afraid. Curious, though."

"Curious about what it would be like to see me naked again?"

Longarm laughed. "Partly, yes."

"And curious to feel what it would be like to make love with me?"

"Mostly that. Damn but you do test a man, don't you?"

She unbuttoned the front of the dress to her waist, and he saw why she had been so cold. She wore nothing under the top of the dress. She pushed the sides of the cloth back to show her breasts.

"Go ahead, meet my big titties. They like company."

She caught one of his hands, pulled it to her chest, and pushed it on her bare breast.

"Yes, that's better. You really want to do me, don't you, Custis?"

He nodded. She grinned, and her hand felt gently at his crotch and found the growing hardness there.

"Yes! I like that. We can at least sit on the bed, so I don't fall over."

She caught his hand, led him to the bed, and sat. She pulled him down beside her. Diane leaned out and kissed his lips, a hard, demanding kiss that let her tongue dart between their open lips.

Her hands worked through his jacket, his sweater, his shirt to his long johns, then to his bare chest.

"Oh, yes!" she said when their lips parted. "I like a man who knows how to kiss a lady." Her other hand rubbed at his crotch, stroking his erection, which showed through his pants.

"Let's get these clothes off and get under the covers so you can get me warmed up until I'm red hot and ready!"

They pulled their clothes off quickly in the freezing room and slid between the covers. Their bodies twined together to stay warm. Her breasts pressed against his chest, and she sighed.

"This is what I dream about on cold nights in my lonely bed," she said softly. He nibbled her ear.

"Whatever you want, however you want it, it's yours. Poke me any place you want to, it's fine with me." She ducked under the covers to his crotch, her open mouth taking him in so far he was sure he'd choke her. She bobbed up and down on his rock-hard erection until he reached down and pulled her up.

"Not there, not this time," he said, his voice rough from the emotion drilling through him. "Too fast that way right now," he said and kissed her and then bent and kissed both her breasts. He came up and stared at her.

"Why did you become a reporter?" Longarm asked.

"So I could go places and meet interesting people. When I found one I liked, I could screw him and move on to another fantastic man in the news."

His hand caressed her breasts, and she growled deep in her throat.

"Don't ever stop doing that. I love to be petted. That's what I was born for. Damn but I love to be loved. Screwing is the best thing a woman ever does. I'd rather be here right now than anywhere on the whole earth."

She turned and in a frenzy kissed him a dozen times, then caught his hand and pulled it down to her crotch. He explored, finger-walked down her leg and then rubbed gently up her soft inner thigh. She began to shiver. He did the same thing again, and then on the other soft, white thigh.

"Touch me, damn you!" she barked. "Touch my cunnie or I'll scream!"

His fingers brushed over her treasure, and she sighed. He stroked past it again, and she caught his hand, holding him there. Slowly he explored, caressed her tender outer lips, and dipped his finger into her glory hole, then came out.

Her breathing was like a steam engine.

He explored a moment more, found her hard clit, and strummed it twice.

"Oh, lordy!" she breathed, barely able to talk. He hit the node half a dozen times, and her hips pounded against him, her breath gushing out in huge gasps. Then the spasms hit her. Diane wailed and moaned as the climax tore through her. Every muscle in her body seemed to contract, and she brayed again as the tremors rattled her, shook her a dozen times before they passed.

She twitched and sighed, and then just before she relaxed they came again, another powerful series of spasms that racked her body and jolted her whole frame shuddering against him, her mouth searching this time for his, her arms clasped around him, and her hips pounding twenty times against his crotch.

The tremors trailed off, her moaning slowed then stopped, and she fell against him so spent and drained that she couldn't even speak for five minutes. He held her as she came back from her mountaintop experience.

"Oh shit! Oh shit! It's never been that wild before. What are you doing to me, Longarm? You haven't even penetrated me yet. God, what's that going to be like?"

She rolled on her back under the covers and pulled him over her, spread her legs and lifted her knees.

"Poke me, damn you, Longarm. Screw me right now or I'm gonna get your six-gun and shoot your balls off!"

Longarm chuckled, eased between her legs, and found her moist, juicy hole with the first thrust. He continued in until their pelvic bones ground together and she let out a huge sigh.

"Perfect! Just the place. Now, this is heaven. I could lay here all day and not even move. Why is screwing so damn wonderful?" She looked at him and then hurried on. "Don't tell me, I know. I just don't want that to happen yet. I'm young. I have plenty of time."

Slowly she began to rotate her hips under him. He countered and moved the other way, multiplying the sexy effect on both of them.

Longarm felt himself surge over that peak where there is no retreat. He pounded into her as hard as he could as the gates unleashed his load and it surged down his tubes and then with one spasmic thrust after another gushed out of him. He felt the thrill of the chase and capture and the coupling all come to one massive and indescribable climax.

He eased down against her and put his head above hers on the bed. Her arms came around him, and she made soft sounds he didn't understand, didn't try to. He felt his breathing slow to near normal as he pulled back from the brink of a small death. She stirred under him for a moment, then tightened her arms to keep him in place.

Ten minutes later she stirred again and let her hands slip apart. He came away from her and lay beside her, tucking the blankets around his shoulders.

"Are you sleepy?" she asked.

"No."

"Good. I hear that older men get sleepy after sex and young men get hungry."

"I'm starved. What time is it?"

"Must be somewhere near noon."

"Let's check with the sheriff's office and then have a bite to eat."

"Maybe two bites. You made me work so hard I'm ready to eat raw a pie-eyed mule."

The sheriff had no reports from the jewelry stores. At their lunch, Diane stared at the deputy marshal.

"Longarm, just what do you think of these two jewel robbers? I mean, who could pull off a robbery like that one? Will it go down in history as one of the best ever done?"

"A clever one, true, but eventually they'll get caught. Almost all outlaws do, you know. The days of the Old West are almost over. We have telegraphs and mail and even pictures to use now in apprehending criminals. We're making it harder and harder for them to survive."

"They must all plan to survive and not get caught."

"True, but once a person steps over that line, on the wrong side of the law, there isn't anything that can save him. That's why I'll catch this pair sooner or later. I can chase as far as they can run."

"To China?"

"Why do you say China?"

"Oh, I don't know. San Francisco and all the ships. Lots of ships go to China. If they get there with the diamonds and other gems, couldn't they live like a king and queen?"

"Yes, China is poor and undeveloped. But first they have to get out of this country."

"And they have to escape from you," she said, eyes glittering. "Will it be hard to capture them?"

"Hard, yes, impossible, no. Now, I'm through eating and you're not. I'm going to abandon you here and go check with the sheriff, then hit all of the jewelry stores again. Think you can find your way back to your hotel?"

"I'll get a local guide if I get lost."

Longarm grinned, took the check, and waved at her. Then he hurried to the cashier, and on to the sheriff's office.

"Had a report," one of the deputies told Longarm as soon as he went in the door. "Johnson Jewelers on Second Street. He said a man about five-ten was in, an old man. He had a letter with a local address on it, so the jeweler figured he was a new resident

94

he didn't know. After the man left, the owner of the shop looked at the letter again. He found nothing but an empty envelope that had been folded several times.

"Then the jeweler read the name again. He knew the man whose name showed on the envelope. The man who sold him the diamond must have found the envelope to use as identification. Thought you'd want to know."

Longarm pulled the collar of his overcoat higher as he walked up the street to Johnson Jewelers. The owner growled a hello when Longarm walked in.

"Yeah, Marshal, I should have recognized the name before. I know that man, he's about thirty, not sixty-five. Damn me! The stone is brilliant. A one-carat blue white, the best-looking stone I've seen in a long time. I paid him a hundred dollars, maybe half what it's worth. Are you gonna take it away from me?"

Longarm explained how he couldn't prove it was part of the stolen goods.

"Just stay on the alert. Probably neither the woman nor the man will try your place again. I'll do the rounds and tell the others about the couple using fake local identification. That will help."

As he made the circuit covering the six other jewelry stores, Longarm passed his hotel, and he hurried up to Kimberly's room. She stood in front of the dresser's wavy mirror combing her hair.

He told her about the new way the robbers had used to sell the gems.

"I want to come with you. I haven't been much help lately. Oh, I got hungry and went down for some lunch. You ready to go? I'll put on my gloves when we get outside."

The cold wind off the street hit them as they turned the corner and walked down another block.

"My guess is that they won't try to sell any more here," Kimberly said. "It seems they're doing it to throw it up in your face as much as anything. Prove that they can get away with it."

Twice that afternoon they circled the jewelry stores, but neither the man nor the woman had tried to sell any more diamonds.

Longarm thought of the bankers, but decided that the pair would not venture into a bank.

He and Kimberly walked into the hotel and pulled off their mittens. They were heading for the big heater when a man hurried over to them from where he had evidently been waiting beside the room clerk's desk.

"Marshal Long?" he asked.

Longarm looked at him and nodded. "Yes. You're a deputy sheriff. Has something happened?"

"Indeed it has, sir. Sheriff sent me to find you. Not a half hour ago those two diamond robbers tried to sell some gems and the store owner tried to sneak out. They stopped him, but a customer escaped.

"Now the robbers have the jeweler and another customer held hostage in the jewelry store. They say if we don't let them leave on the next train, they'll do something drastic."

Longarm turned with the deputy sheriff and ran for the front door.

"Stay here," he ordered Kimberly and rushed outside, following the deputy sheriff.

They both settled into a jog and two blocks later came up to the store. Longarm checked out the sheriff's men. One stood with a rifle near a post across the street. A second deputy hunkered down beside the front door, with his back against the outside wall. The windows in the jewelry store were all intact. The sheriff walked from a store on the same side of the street as the jeweler.

The lawman nodded at Longarm. "We got 'em for you, Marshal. All you need to do is go in and bring them out."

"Sounds easy enough. You have a man on the back door in the alley?"

"Got a good man back there."

"Send another one, farther out, as a backup. These people are experts at their trade."

The sheriff frowned for a moment, but turned and yelled at a deputy, who ran through a store toward the alley.

"Who's the second hostage?" Longarm asked.

"The hardware man from across the street. In there chewing the rag if I know Homer."

"We gonna rush 'em, Sheriff?" a deputy asked.

"Up to Longarm, his case."

"We won't rush them with two hostages inside," Longarm said. "How did they tell you about the train?"

"Woman opened a window and yelled," the deputy said.

A moment later Longarm saw the window open again. They were two stores down, watching from a doorway. He edged closer until he was at the front of the jewelry store, just out of sight beside the big window.

"Longarm, you out there yet?" a woman's voice bellowed.

"Waiting to hear from you, Riane. Looks like you're in a heap of trouble."

"Not a damn bit, Longarm. We've got two hostages in here. Unless you do exactly as I say, they're shot bloody dead and gone to hell before you can blink your eyes."

Chapter 11

Longarm listened to the jewel robber's threats and snorted. "Lady you've got it wrong. I don't give a didley damn about those two hostages. You blow them into hell and you've got no cover at all. We blast that store into pieces and you and Heinrich with it. What kind of chances you think you'll have then?"

"You're bluffing, Longarm. You're a deputy U.S. marshal, and you don't let hostages die. Here's what we want. There's a work train coming in here from the Union Pacific line in a little over half an hour that's carrying two passenger cars to make up for missed schedules due to the snow.

"It'll come in, let off passengers, and head right back to the junction with the main line. We'll be on it. You bring a closed carriage for four to the front door now. Drive it right up on the boardwalk. We get in it and go to the depot and board that train. If any messages are sent on the telegraph, both our hostages get head-shot. You listening to me, Longarm?"

"I'm listening. Just don't see how you could be so smart in Chicago and so stupid here. You've got no place to run. There's two feet of snow out here and more west. You've got a westbound train and lots of telegraph time before you get to the next station, where they seal the car and strip-search everyone until they find you. Not a chance in hell of getting away."

A six-gun shot jolted into the quiet of the Salt Lake City late afternoon. A scream of pain was bellowed from the jewelry store's partly open window.

Riane Moseley's voice came again.

"Hear that, Longarm? One of the hostages just back-talked to Eric and got shot in the leg as a warning. Works for you, too. Now get that carriage up here. The train will be along in less than a half hour."

Longarm talked with the sheriff.

"Best do as she says," the county lawman said. "I don't cotton to having two dead merchants on my hands. Town won't stand for that."

"You know about that special mixed work train?"

"First I've heard of it. Happens now and then, especially after bad snowstorms."

"Have one of your deputies check it out. Meantime we better get a carriage. Can you locate one fast?"

"Yep. The livery has one for rent. I'll have a man get it. Tell her. I don't want either of those men killed."

Longarm went back to the front of the jewelry store.

"Riane, you win this skirmish. The sheriff is bringing a carriage up."

"About time. Don't worry, the train is coming. I want you to clear the street between here and the train station. Not a soul on the boardwalk or in the street. You hear that, Sheriff?"

"He heard you," Longarm said.

"You, Mr. United States Deputy Marshal, I want you to lead the team of horses from here to the station. Know that I'll have a shotgun trained on you every step of the way. One signal, one miscue, and your badge will be bloody and soon pinned on another man, one who is still alive. You understand, Longarm?"

"I just got to cough and marvel at the way you got with words, Miss Moseley. But remember this is just one small battle, not the whole war. I'll be on that train as well. You can count on it."

"You get on the train, both the hostages die, Longarm. They're coming with us for insurance. Don't do anything stupid."

"Robbery might get you ten years, Riane. You shoot those men and you both will hang, that's a promise."

99

"Promises are easy to make and damn hard to carry out."

Longarm pulled away from the window. The sheriff had sent a dozen deputies out to clear the streets of the gawkers and curious.

"Sheriff, do you have a sharpshooter on your staff? Somebody who can shoot the eyes out of a gopher at thirty yards?"

"Thought about that, Longarm. Trouble is he could get one of them, but not both. Have to kill them both to save our two men. Can you justify that?"

"No judge in the land would even let that go to trial, Sheriff. Trouble is getting them both at once, and not hitting the hostages."

"Have to do it as they try to get in the carriage," the sheriff said.

"We could have a man inside the carriage waiting for them, but that would be suicide. Don't get the carriage too close to the door."

"Don't think we can get a team of horses that will walk on those planks. Most animals get spooky on the boards."

"Good," Longarm said. "Give us more of a chance to nail them. She won't like it, but I'll have to convince her."

He saw the buggy coming down the street. The driver of the rig tried once to get the horses onto the boardwalk where it was only six inches off the street. Both animals balked at the rise.

Longarm went into the street and waved the rig on down so it stopped sideways to the jewelry store, at the edge of the ten-foot-wide boardwalk. They had cleared a wagon and three horses away from the walk to make room for the carriage.

Longarm kept his six-gun in leather and walked up to the front of the store.

"Riane, best we can do. The horses wouldn't jump up the foot to get on the boardwalk. Most animals hate walking on boards this way. Don't trust them. Close as we can get. Next move is up to you."

"Figured you'd try that, Longarm. One thing you ain't is stupid. So here's what I want. No lawman in sight, not a one except you. No sharpshooters in windows or doors, or we blast one of these hostages into hell. You hear me?"

"I understand."

"All right. When we come out, I'll have my .45 derringer in the ear of the jeweler. You try and head-shoot me, and my reflexes will fire that trigger and you'll have a dead ring salesman. Eric will have his six-gun under the chin of the other man. Just the slightest try at stopping us, and both these men die. I'm sure the sheriff doesn't want that. Are we clear?"

"Clear as the Mississippi River, Riane. You really expect to get away on the train?"

"Absolutely. Unless the county wants two of its merchants blown into bits. Now get rid of the hack driver. You lead those horses on foot to the station. No chance for a runaway. Don't get smart, or people start dying, you first of all."

Longarm went out to the carriage and had the driver tie the reins loosely. Then the man ran into a store on the other side of the street.

Longarm waved at the jewelry store, and a figure eased out the door. It was the jeweler, and he had his arms around an old lady with gray hair in a long purple dress, carrying a leather valise in one hand and holding a derringer in the ear of the jeweler with the other.

The hostage backed up as the pair worked slowly toward the buggy. She got in first, ramming the derringer into the jeweler's gut, then pulling him inside.

The man came out next with a chokehold on the second hostage and a six-gun pressed against the man's head. He, too, carried a leather valise. Evidently the two robbers had all of the jewels with them if they were ready to leave town. For just a moment Longarm wanted to turn, draw, and fire. Sacrifice the two lives to get the robbers.

A moment later a shotgun fired in the air over his head.

"Don't even think about it, Lawman," Riane barked. "If he goes down, you're the next one, then anyone I can see on the street."

Longarm swore softly as the tall man shuffled forward with the hardware store owner, until both of them crawled into the carriage.

"Move it," Riane called, and Longarm caught the halter of the lead horse and walked at his normal gait down the street. It was four blocks to the train station. The deputies had worked wonders, and no one was on the streets or even looking out of store windows.

That was the toughest four-block walk of U.S. Deputy Marshal Long's life.

When they were a block from the station, Longarm heard a train whistle, evidently from the arriving engine. So far today all of his luck had been bad.

"Move up as close as you can to the tracks." Riane's voice boomed from the carriage. Longarm looked back but couldn't spot her in the rig. By this time dusk had settled in, and he could see lamps burning in some of the stores and houses.

The engine arrived in the station with a steaming entrance, and behind it Longarm saw two work cars and two passenger types. A dozen people stepped off the two cars; then Riane called to Longarm.

"Run up to the conductor and tell him the situation. He's to depart as soon as we're on board, regardless of his schedule. If he doesn't, the two hostages and then a few of the train crew will start to die. It's up to him."

Longarm caught the conductor just as the last of the people left the first car. He explained the situation and showed his badge.

"Not a lot we can do right now," Longarm said. "I hope to have the situation in hand before we get to the main line."

"You better. We're just the spur run. The boys down at Union Pacific won't take kindly to anything like this."

"We'll have it resolved long before then," Longarm said. The conductor scowled and went toward the station.

"Oh, no telegrams to the other end. Specific instructions from the robbers."

The trainman shrugged. "I tried."

By that time, the two robbers and their hostages were nearly to the train. Longarm saw no sign of any of the sheriff's men. Good. So far nobody had been killed.

The guns were still in place, pressing into the hostages as the group of four walked up to the first passenger car. When she was up the steps, Riane looked at the conductor.

"I want all of the passengers you have heading for points north to get into this first car. You understand me, Conductor?"

"Yes, ma'am. Won't be many, maybe fifteen or twenty."

He nodded and stepped back and welcomed the passengers as they came on.

A half hour later, the train was in the same spot in the station. Riane looked out the window at the conductor and motioned to him.

He came inside.

"Why aren't we moving?" she asked.

"The engineer says he won't move the train as long as there are robbers on board."

Riane went to the door of the train, leaned out, and fired a six-gun round off the side of the engine. There was no reaction. She fired again, hitting the smokestack.

This time the engineer looked out his window.

"Tell him if he doesn't move us at once, you get a .45 slug through your left eye."

The conductor paled, ran down the steps, and waved both arms toward the front of the rig. He yelled something at the engineer, and the train gushed out a cloud of pent-up steam and edged forward.

Longarm lay flat on top of the first passenger car. He had crawled up there while Riane argued with the conductor. Now he saw her come out on the vestibule with her six-gun waving. She must have been wondering where Longarm had gone. She leaned out and scanned the train cars as they picked up speed. He wondered what she would do next. He couldn't take the chance of capturing her now and putting the lives of the two hostages in jeopardy from Heinrich.

He could shoot her now, but he had no chance to capture her without her using her gun. That would alert Heinrich. Before he had decided on any other course of action, she stepped back into the first car.

Longarm walked as quietly as he could down the top of the first passenger car to the end of it. She had all the people in the first car. Why? He knew before he had to think about it. She would change her costume and makeup in the second car and become another face lost in the crowd.

Maybe he could interrupt her. He swung down the ladder on the side of the car and stepped into the vestibule. As he looked through the heavy glass into the first car, he saw about twenty passengers. Where was Riane? She had had plenty of time to slip into the second car, use it as her dressing room, and walk back into this one when no one would notice.

The night lights were on in the car, but they were dim. The car was unheated, but some of the passengers had taken off the heavy coats they'd worn to the train. He might not recognize Riane now even if she hadn't changed her disguise. How could he stop twenty people and search them and make sure they were not the robbers?

He stepped into the first car and walked up the aisle, looking closely at every small woman he found. Most of them seemed to be small this time. Some were obviously too old and had brown eyes to prove they were not Riane Moseley.

Five-three, blue eyes, hair color uncertain, slender, pretty—that was his robber woman.

He arrived at the far end of the car without finding a single good suspect for the girl. The man was just as hard to tag. Where were they? With a chill, he remembered that he hadn't seen the two hostages either. He eased his Colt in its leather and hurried to the second car. He stepped through the connecting doors into the vestibule, then into the second passenger car.

As he opened the door leading to the seats, he faced the deadly twin barrels of a sawed-off shotgun, an old woman and an elderly man. Both laughed when he couldn't keep the surprise from surging onto his face.

"Thought we'd change our disguises?" Riane asked. "Why do that? These outfits have worked well so far. Now a federal marshal is going to have an accident falling off the train. Won't that be too bad. Might break his neck. First a few things to get done."

Longarm saw the two hostages with hands tied in front of them sitting in the second row of seats. He looked directly at them.

"You men all right?"

The jeweler glanced up and nodded. The hardware man pointed to a makeshift bandage on his leg. "I need a doctor to dig out the slug," he said. "Hurts like hell. All these two do is laugh."

"Maybe you'd laugh, too, if you had three hundred thousand dollars' worth of diamonds, rubies, and emeralds in your kit bag," Marshal Long said.

Heinrich scowled at Longarm. "Those people can't count right. At the top we have about a hundred thousand dollars' worth. They put in exaggerated claims so the insurance company will pay. People do it all the time reporting a theft of their jewels."

"A mere hundred thousand? Doesn't seem like enough to kill two hostages for," Longarm said.

"That's why they're still alive," Riane said, and for moment Longarm caught the same little twist of her mouth that had looked familiar when he'd seen it before. The way she smiled, then scowled, with nothing in between. He had it, and he wasn't at all happy.

"Well, if it isn't Diane Snook, girl reporter. You haven't changed much," Longarm said.

Riane Moseley laughed and stared at him. "I sure had you fooled, though, didn't I? You couldn't tell me from Eve until you had this close-up look. I think I put on a damn good performance."

"You did, Riane. You were fantastic in bed. Does Eric know about our afternoon of sexual ecstasy?"

She glanced at Eric, then looked back at Longarm. "Of course. It was his idea. We had to find out how much you knew about us."

"I know enough, a lot more than I told you."

"You told us more than we needed. If that bastard of a jeweler hadn't tried to play hero, we would have been away clean and perfect again."

"Can't expect to get a hit every time you come up to bat in the baseball game."

"Not many do." She laughed now. "But I get more hits than anyone else." Her face turned sober. "Now ease that six-gun out of your holster and lay it on the floor, ever so slow."

Longarm couldn't fight against a sawed-off mankiller. He did as she instructed him.

"Now sit down on the floor with your back to the wall over there by the front seat. Do it slow and easy and no tricks, or my widow maker here will blow you right through the side of the train car."

"You've got the high hand. Enjoy the feeling while you can." Longarm eased down to the floor and put his elbows on his bent-up knees.

"Now, that's much better. The three of you be quiet now and rest up. You might need to do some walking soon. Longarm, have you ever jumped off a train doing thirty-five miles an hour in the mountains and in the dark?"

"Once or twice."

"Good. The practice might help you. The four of you sit tight. I'm going to go up to the other end of the car and make some small adjustments." She stopped in front of Longarm. "Oh, Custis, one thing you haven't seen about me. My real hair. I don't have gray hair or long red hair. You must have figured that out by now." She laughed and went out of his sight down the aisle.

Eric Heinrich now held the shotgun. Longarm figured the girl wouldn't blow them to bits, but this Heinrich just might. Longarm didn't like the look in his eyes. They were angry eyes. Angry men often did strange things.

Longarm settled down to think what to do. He had them almost in his grasp; all he had to do was figure out how to capture them without a lot of blood being spilled—including his own.

His mind surveyed the possibilities, none of which seemed practical: attack Heinrich, jump off the train, throw Heinrich off the train, stop the train, and, use the derringer in the enlarged watch pocket of his vest.

The hideout was the best possibility, but when and how? Take Heinrich now and tie him up and get the girl when she boiled up here shooting? How could he keep the two hostages from getting slaughtered?

Too damn many questions.

Whatever he was going to do, he had to make it fast, while the two were split up. He worked one hand slowly under his overcoat.

Heinrich looked at him and swung around a six-gun with a short barrel. He had put the shotgun on the seat near where he stood.

"What the hell you doing, Lawman?"

"Just trying to get this damn overcoat off," Longarm said.

"Leave it on. It might cushion your fall when you go out the door," Heinrich growled.

Longarm worked his hand into his vest and pulled out the .44–40 derringer soldered to the watch chain on his vest. He pulled the watch out as well, so he could swing up the weapon easier. All of this was hidden by his overcoat.

Heinrich stood four feet from him, glowering at the two hostages.

"I didn't like the idea of bringing these two chunks of meat. Should have shot them back there. I told Riane they would be trouble." Heinrich held the six-gun at his side and looked down the aisle.

"Woman, ain't you ever coming back?" he shouted.

Just then, Longarm pulled out the derringer and fired twice at the back of Heinrich's hand holding the six-gun.

Chapter 12

The twin blasts from the .44–40 derringer sounded like a cannon in the train car. Both rounds jolted through the robber's hand, smashing the weapon from his fingers. It dropped to the floor and skittered out of reach. Heinrich staggered backward and fell onto the first seat.

"Down behind the seats!" Longarm barked at the two hostages. He dove forward, grabbed the dropped six-gun, and rolled behind the first chairs, opposite the wounded jewel robber.

"Eric, what happened back there?" Riane's voice shouted from the rear of the car forty feet away.

Longarm saw the shotgun where it lay on the first seat across the aisle. Heinrich moved toward it. Longarm fired again into the cushion near Heinrich, and he stopped. The deputy U.S. marshal surged across the aisle, grabbed the shotgun, and dove back to the far side.

As he passed the aisle the second time, a handgun fired from down the car, but the slug missed him and clanged into the metal of the car door.

Longarm untied the hostages' hands. Heinrich had a wound on his leg where one of the rounds must have hit him after going through his hand. He held his bleeding hand and glared at Longarm.

"Might as well give it up, Riane," Longarm called. "I have Eric, his valise, the shotgun, and his six-gun. You're short on weapons and out of luck."

A hot lead round answered him, hitting the front of the car an inch over the back of the last seat. It ricocheted off the metal door and stopped when it cracked the window opposite Longarm.

Longarm loaded the derringer and slid it back in place, put his watch in the pocket and checked the aisle. There were twenty seats between him and the woman. He lunged down the opening between the seats and dove behind the third one. No shot came from Riane.

For a moment he worried about not having checked Heinrich for a hideout, but the man didn't look like the type who would carry one. What could Riane do? She wouldn't give up and turn herself in. She'd try something, but what? Just then the train slowed. It would be coming into some small settlement between Salt Lake City and the main line. Longarm didn't remember stopping anywhere coming down.

She might get off!

Longarm surged ahead for three more seats before ducking behind one of them. This time he drew fire, her handgun drumming a round into the back of the seat he had just left.

"You'll have to do better than that," he chided her when the booming sound of the shot faded away.

"Bastard! You weren't supposed to be this good. You can keep Eric. I don't need him anymore."

The train slowed more, and Longarm could see a few lights in buildings along the tracks. He surged another three seats forward and ducked behind one of the heavy upholstered benches.

No reaction from Riane.

The train's brakes took hold, and it came to a gentle stop. Longarm looked around the edge of the seat. He was halfway to the end. She'd have to go through the inside door to the vestibule to get off the car.

He waited. The train's whistle hooted.

Longarm turned and shouted to the hostages. "Jeweler, tie up that man with the bloody hand. Both of you sit on him and hold him for the authorities. I may have to leave you."

109

As he looked back, he saw the door out of the car half-open. He snapped a shot that missed, and the girl vanished through the door.

Longarm raced down the aisle, the six-gun in his right hand, the sawed-off scattergun in his left. He pulled open the door and looked. Clear. He went down the steps to the snow-covered platform.

A six-gun blasted to his left, and he felt the slug tear into his heavy overcoat and graze his left arm. As soon as he hit the planks, he raced toward the woman. She carried only the valise and the weapon. She darted into a group of people coming toward the train, and for a moment he lost her. Half a dozen men and women had come to welcome someone, and by the time Longarm hurried through them, Riane had vanished.

The station house was too far away.

She wasn't with the people he had just come past.

The only other cover was the train itself. The train whistle sounded and steam hissed as the engineer applied power. The driver wheels spun on the rails until they could grab traction, and the heavy train inched forward like a long snake.

Did she get on the train or go through to the ground on the other side?

The first passenger car steps were opposite him now. Longarm raced for them and caught hold, went up them and down the other side to look out. There was nothing but pristine white snow along the tracks. Anyone leaving by that way would make a big mark in the snow, visible even in the dark.

She was still on the train.

Longarm entered the car with the passengers and checked each one. He found her sitting almost at the end of the car, the valise between her feet, under her skirt and almost hidden. She sat in the forward-facing seat and had pushed the back of the seat across from her to the other side, to rest her feet on the cushion.

This time she had blond hair, cut short, and he saw that there was no room now for a wig. It was her real hair.

That soft little smile came, and he knew she was Riane. She held one hand in her reticule, and he figured it gripped a derringer.

He slid into the seat beside her, his Colt pressing against her side.

"So, the chase is over," Longarm said. He nodded at the reticule. "What was it you said about reflex action? If you shoot me, my finger will spasm and pull the trigger, and you'll be dead for sure. Your aim with that peashooter might not be so good."

"I'll have to take that risk, if I decide that's the best thing to do."

She looked at him then, with that great smile she had, and it made him grin, remembering her in bed. She had taken off all of the makeup that made her look old. Her skin was clean and glowing with the promise of youth and innocence.

"I don't suppose my offer of half the diamonds would convince you to put down your gun?"

"You suppose correctly. I wouldn't know what to do with all that stolen money."

"I could help you figure it out, in San Francisco or Mexico City, even China."

"Afraid not. I heard somebody say we're only about twenty minutes from the end of the line."

"Not the end of my line. This game between us of cat and mouse ain't over until it's all finished. I'm far from finished. What is it they call this, a Mexican standoff?"

"Not quite. I've got the bigger gun, faster hands. I knock your reticule away and it's really over."

He brought the shotgun up and laid it on his lap so it pointed at her stomach. He cocked the hammer.

"Now, Riane, is the game over?"

The train jolted as the brakes went on and the wheels locked and skidded. They had been sitting in the forward-facing seat, and both were thrown forward by the sudden deceleration. The shotgun fell, but Longarm grabbed it before it hit the floor and discharged.

He saw the reticule fly out of Riane's hand as she tried to catch herself on the other seat. A moment later they landed half on the seat and half on the floor, in a confusing mass of flailing arms and legs.

Longarm tried to block her. She scrambled onto the seat, jumped over his outstretched hand, and stepped into the aisle.

They were only four rows from the entrance to the car. By the time Longarm got untangled and lunged into the aisle, the woman had vanished through the car door. He left the shotgun and charged after her.

The half door at the bottom of the steps hung open, and beyond it lay only a blur of green trees covered with white and a foot of snow on the ground.

In the moonlight, he saw her tracks. They went straight to the trees less than forty feet down the right-of-way-slope and into the woods.

Without a brilliant thought to push him, Longarm jumped from the train, pulled his overcoat around him, and charged into the snow.

A shot from the woods boomed in the silence; then he heard the trainmen swearing as they released the emergency braking devices and got the train ready to move again. He'd seen it happen before. Someone had pulled the emergency cord, locking the brakes in place. It would take them twenty minutes to get under way again, after a lot of sweat and swearing.

The shot missed him, and he centered on the sound, kicking snow as he tried to run. He gave up and took big steps, following the the less widely spaced footprints in the snow ahead of him. Longarm veered off the trail and ran into the woods twenty feet from where Riane had entered it. No chance for a bushwhacking that way.

Once in the trees, he found the ground bare of snow. He stopped and listened. For a moment he heard nothing. Then a squirrel scratched up a tree, a bird fluted some night song a hundred yards away, small feral feet scampered through the leaves and pine needles.

Then he heard a new sound—larger feet, noisy ones, moving to the right through the woods. He'd learned years ago how to negotiate any kind of woods without a sound. Now he did so, six-gun in hand, not breaking a branch or letting a limb swish back as he moved toward the girl's footfalls. No one else would be in this place; it had to be her.

Her footsteps stopped. Longarm stopped, too, waiting, listening.

An owl, with its peculiar wing sound, whistled out of a tree some distance ahead. She had flushed it out. Her steps began again, and she ran.

He ran toward her. In the sparse pine woods it was half-light where the moon shone through the trees. There was little brush here.

Longarm increased his speed and then stopped, hugging a pine. The girl's steps were still ahead, veering to the left. He angled that way, running fast now through fewer trees and more light.

He saw her ahead, looking back. She fired a shot that went wide. Had she reloaded? Would she have had any spare rounds with her? He sprinted from tree to tree now for some cover. He gained on her, and even in the thicker woods he could spot her. She slowed. He gained quickly, and then she fell. She came to her knees, then sagged to the ground.

From ten feet Longarm peered at her around a pine. The six-gun was aimed toward him. The first round hit the tree. When she tried to fire again, the hammer fell on a spent round or an empty chamber.

Longarm stepped out from behind the tree.

"Now I'd say the game is over, Riane."

"Not exactly." She pulled the trigger again, and the gun fired. The round tore into his shoulder. It had been slowed by his heavy overcoat but still had enough power to drive him back two steps. He knew the round had penetrated flesh, but there was little pain. He could feel blood running down his arm. Longarm slumped behind the tree, his six-gun still in his hand.

"You forgot about the old empty chamber trick, Longarm." She stood, took a deep breath, and turned away from him. Longarm fired twice with the Colt. The second round smashed into her right leg, and she went down, her weapon jolting out of her hand and into a patch of light snow.

Longarm ran up and grabbed the revolver, then felt under her coat, checking for any other weapons. He found the derringer he had seen her with before, and a knife in her reticule.

He tied her hands together behind her back, then looked at her leg. Riane screamed when he moved her foot.

"Broken," he said. "I'll put some splints around it and tie them tight, then get you to a doctor." He gathered some fallen branches, broke them with his boot against a downed log, and brought over two the right size. He used her scarf and his kerchief and tied the inch-thick branches around her leg. She bleated in agony. Not even the freezing cold could numb the pain.

He moved his right arm. He could feel the blood, but the shoulder didn't seem to be hurt much. He'd look at it later.

Riane couldn't walk. He carried her for a hundred yards, then put her down near a tree. So far he'd seen nothing but trees and snow. He guessed they had been paralleling the tracks. He climbed a small hill and looked north. Twin lights in a window greeted him.

Twenty minutes later he eased Riane onto a bed in the small ranch house and thanked the owners.

The Hostetlers said they lived a mile from the little town called Deweyville.

"Sure, the train goes through here, but usually it don't stop," Mr. Hostetler said. "The south night train comes with the mail, I guess."

Longarm checked his watch. A little before eight P.M. "Mr. Hostetler, do you have a horse we could borrow to get to town? This lady has a broken leg and it needs mending."

"Horse and a buggy, but don't think the road is open yet. Do have a sleigh fit for two. You want me to roust it out?"

Longarm said he did. He checked the small bandage he had put over the bullet hole in Riane's leg. It had stopped the bleeding. He couldn't set a broken leg.

It took them a half hour to get the horse hitched to the sleigh and the runners unfrozen from the snow. Then the vehicle was up and ready. Longarm bundled Riane into the sleigh with a comforter from Mrs. Hostetler. He promised to leave it, the sleigh, and the horse in town, at the blacksmith shop. They didn't have a livery stable there.

The directions had been precise, and Longarm pulled the rig up in front of the resident physician a little before nine o'clock. It took three hard raps on the door to get the doctor out of his comfortable chair.

He let them in his small office and examined the leg wound. "Yep, seems to be a problem here. Have it fixed up in no time."

"Doctor, is the telegraph man still on duty at the railroad station?"

"Yep, got a man on all night now, a block over to the north. The night work train came through twenty minutes ago, so you missed it."

Longarm hurried over and sent a wire to the Union Pacific agent at the junction ahead, asking him to have a law officer hold Eric Heinrich, who should be coming in from Salt Lake City wounded in the hand and the leg by gunfire. He was a fugitive and under arrest for jewel robbery.

Longarm hurried back to the doctor's place and knocked, then let himself in at the office door. The doctor had just washed up and was about to leave.

"Doctor, how is the lady and her broken leg?" Longarm asked.

The medic looked at him with a frown. "Broken leg? No such thing. She had a bullet wound that went right through. Missed the bone by near an inch. Nice little lady you got there. She said to tell you she'd meet you at the station and wait for the next train through."

"Oh, damn," Longarm said. "Did she pay you?"

"Right, five dollars. Usual I don't get paid in cash that way. I'll have to report the gunshot wound, but she gave me her name and address in Salt Lake City. Accident with a handgun, she said."

"She would." Longarm didn't bother to thank the doctor. He surged out the clinic door and raced for the train station. Then he stopped. That was the last place she would be. Where would she hide out until the next train came through? Some spot she could stay warm and see the station.

He checked the small business district. There were two cafes, one still open. He looked through the window, then went in and asked the waitress if Riane had been in. The waitress said that she hadn't.

Longarm walked the street end to end but could see no spot where she might be. There wasn't a saloon in town, this being a highly Mormon area.

She had probably walked up to some house with lights on, and with her best acting talent talked them into giving her shelter for the night. Which house might it be? Impossible to find her. He couldn't check every house in town.

He went back to the cafe. It was open until eleven o'clock. The town had no hotel. He'd have a good meal and stay there until the place closed. When had he eaten last? At noon? He wasn't sure.

When eleven o'clock came, he went to the train station and talked his way into the telegraph operator's small office, where he stoked the wood burning stove. At least he could stay warm until the next train to the north came through. That wouldn't be until a little after nine o'clock the next morning.

He sent a telegram to Kimberly in Salt Lake City and requested the wire be delivered on arrival without fail.

"Kimberly Walkenhorst, Sunrise Hotel, Salt Lake City. Took the work train out of Salt Lake about dusk, yesterday. Robbers on board. Caught them, lost them. Now stranded at Deweyville about ten miles from the junction with the Union Pacific. You be on the morning train out of Salt Lake at 6 A.M. and bring my traveling bag. Have neither robber in custody . . . yet."

He signed it "Longarm," and the operator sent it humming down the wires.

Sometime after midnight, Longarm dozed. When he came awake, he felt something hard and cold pressing into the side of his neck. His eyes blinked open, and he saw Eric Heinrich's grinning face.

Riane stood to one side with a gun aimed at the telegraph operator.

"Well, our big bad U.S. marshal is awake. Good. That'll make it more fun."

"Where were you?"

"Hiding. Eric got off the train when it came through, figuring I'd show up here. He bashed those merchants and got away from them easy. That doctor even tied up his hand and his leg. Eric saw you bring me into town and came into the medic's office as soon as you left."

"You're still a long way from San Francisco."

"Not all that far, without you chasing us. Now all we have to do is decide just exactly how we're going to shoot you full of holes without killing you.

"I prefer to blast apart both your knees, but Eric is more partial to one knee and both elbows. We have lots of time to decide. Nearly eight hours before our train pulls in. Eight hours is going to seem like forever the way you're going to be hurting, big, tough U.S. Deputy Marshal Custis Long."

Chapter 13

In the small telegrapher's office where the two robbers held Longarm and the keyman at gunpoint, the key chattered again and again. The man who worked there automatically moved to the instrument. Heinrich rammed his six-gun upward under his chin.

"Touch it and you die," Heinrich spat.

"If he doesn't answer that request, his boss will wonder what's happened up here and send somebody to investigate," Longarm said. He paused as if thinking about it. "Ayuh, after I ponder on it a bit, I guess it's best just not to answer the call."

The telegrapher looked at Longarm in a panic. The gunman moved the revolver away.

"Yeah. That's what you think, Longarm. You think I'm stupid. Answer it, but don't try no tricks."

The small man with the green eyeshade, who'd told Longarm when they first met that his name was Toby, moved his hand to the key and tapped out a response. Longarm knew enough code to catch the gist of the incoming message. It had been a routine clearance for all night wires.

The man with the eyeshade then sent out a code word used for emergencies and asking for help. The key remained silent for a moment, then a flood of queries came in on the machine.

"Hey, what the hell?" Heinrich blurted. "Why is that thing going crazy all of a sudden?"

"Just routine," Toby said. "That's what we do on this thing, send and receive messages, remember."

Heinrich started to club Toby with his six-gun, but Riane touched his arm and stopped him.

"Let's all just settle down and get through the next few hours. First I want to get some rest; then we'll figure out exactly what to do with Longarm. Telegraph man, you have nothing to fear from us. We're interested only in Longarm here and the next train north."

"Should be in about nine in the morning," Toby said.

The chattering came again, and the small man bent over his pad of paper, writing down the message. When it was over, he looked at the others.

"Bad news. That was a report from a little flag stop south about twenty miles. There's been a bad avalanche and rock slide. The tracks are covered up. The man there said it would take two days to clear the tracks. Doesn't look like we'll be having a morning train out of Salt Lake get this far up the tracks after all."

Longarm stared at the keyman, who turned so the other two couldn't see him and winked. It was a blatant lie by the telegrapher, hoping it might help somehow.

"Well, looks like we're stranded here for a while," Longarm said. "Maybe they'll send in an engine from the main line."

"Can't do that," Toby said, shaking his head. "We're a little outfit, only have the three steam engines. Them damn things cost a lot. One is in the shop for repairs, and the other two are both down in Salt Lake City right now."

"Damn! We are stuck here," Heinrich bellowed. "I knew we should have charged straight through to San Francisco. I never wanted to come down here just so we could rub it in Longarm's face. Told you that, dammit!"

"Shut up, Eric," Riane snapped. "We've got enough problems without fighting between ourselves. Let's just figure out how to get out of here. Keyman, what about the wagon road from here to the main line?"

"Snowed full. Doubt if a saddle horse could even get through.

More than three feet of snow and drifts up to six foot. Snowed hard here most of yesterday."

"Under the trees there isn't much snow," Riane said. "We can get a pair of horses and try it. Better than being snowed in here for two days."

Longarm still sat on the floor, where he had been when they awakened him. He shifted his position, and Heinrich jolted the side of his six-gun into Longarm's shoulder.

"Don't move, bastard. I still owe you for this hand. Oh, don't worry, I can shoot left-handed just fine. Right now I'll take that six-gun of yours and your hideout. You fooled me with it once, but not again."

He slid the Colt out of leather, pushed Longarm's overcoat and jacket aside, and pulled the watch chain, watch, and the .44–40 derringer from the enlarged vest pocket.

"Damn but that's a little one," Heinrich said. "I'll be using that tiny pistol myself."

He went back to Toby, who had been writing down messages from the chattering key and sending now and then. Longarm tried to hear the outgoing. One was to Salt Lake City about the takeover of the station there in Deweyville and the fact that there was a U.S. deputy marshal captured as well. Toby also requested that a special engine with some sheriff deputies come down from the Main Line station.

Longarm knew that no help could arrive in time. If they were going to get out of this, he and Toby had to do it. An idea started to form. He called to the small man at the desk.

"Toby, maybe you could ask the Union Pacific to send in a rescue engine and one car. They might just do it to help out."

Toby looked up, and his slight frown was replaced with a nod. "Yeah, they did it before, when we had a bad slide two years ago. I'll get a request off right now." He tapped on the key without even a look for permission from Heinrich.

They waited a few minutes, and then the key dot-and-dashed again. Longarm picked up the destination of the message. It was going to somewhere in California. That didn't stop Toby. He wrote down a message in block letters and grinned.

"The Union Pacific in Rock Springs say they can send in an engine and one rescue car from the main junction. That's about twenty miles north. Should be here in less than an hour."

"Will they know to stop here for instructions?" Longarm asked.

"Why stop here if they're going to the avalanche?" Riane asked.

Toby looked at her. "They always establish an O.B. near the trouble site. That's train talk for Operations Base. Then they send out the rescue rig and keep in communications."

"That U.P. engineer won't know this area, will he?" Longarm asked.

Toby shook his head. "Not a chance. We'll have to station somebody outside to flag down the train. For that we use a two-foot white flag on a pole."

"You don't leave that key," Riane said to Toby. "I want to know what's going on all the time."

"I'll go," Longarm said.

Heinrich snorted. "Sure you would, and just keep running. I'll do it. Where's the damn flag?"

Toby got it for him from a closet. "Just stand on the platform, and when you see the headlamp on the train, wave your flag side to side so he can see you down the tracks. Takes a while to stop one of them big engines."

Heinrich hovered near the wood-burning heater. "When do I go out?"

"Now," Riane said. "We don't want it to go rolling right past us. We'll talk them into taking us back to the main line on their first return trip."

Heinrich growled and swore as he went out the door into the wind that had sprung up and whipped around the small station with a numbing whine.

Riane stood by the fire, holding the six-gun in her right hand.

"How's that broken leg of yours?" Longarm asked her.

She laughed. "Fooled you on that one, didn't I? Just some of my acting tools of the trade. I've never been shot before, and I can tell you that bullet hole hurts like hell. Didn't you pick up a wound or two back there?"

"One in my right shoulder that I could get along without."

"Tough. You should have had that doctor fix it."

"As a gentleman, I let you use his services first."

"Too bad." She looked from one of the men to the other. "What? Now I suppose you want me to bandage your shoulder. Not a chance. I'm no doctor."

" 'Pears like we have time," Toby said. "He did get you to the doctor, from what you said. Just be a natural kindness."

"Kindness? This marshal is trying to arrest me and throw me in prison. You want me to think about kindness toward him?"

"I figured you wouldn't help him," Toby said. "Lots of times the prettier a woman is, the more selfish and self-centered and hard to live with she is."

"Live with? You don't even know me."

"Personal experience with two other women. I got me a plain woman now, and she's the kindest soul I ever met."

Riane walked around the stove, glared at both the men, and at last gave in.

"All right, Longarm, take off your coat and let's see that bullet wound. Can't be all that bad the way you've been charging around."

She started to clean the wound—a quarter-inch furrow in his arm just below the shoulder—with some alcohol. Toby stepped up beside her and whacked her alongside the head with a piece of firewood. She gave a little cry and clutched at Longarm; then her eyes snapped closed and she sagged to the floor, unconscious.

"Great work, Toby. We may get out of this mess yet." Longarm grabbed his six-gun from where she had put it, then searched her for weapons and found the derringer and a six-gun in her reticule. He looked in the leather valise she still carried. It wasn't large, and inside he found more diamonds and unset gems than he had ever seen.

All of it or half? He'd find out. He emptied the gems into a small cardboard box Toby gave him and pushed it onto the top shelf against the back wall.

Longarm tied her hands behind her back with some cord Toby got for him. He made sure the knots were solid. Then he tied her ankles together.

A short time later, Riane came awake slowly and with a groan. She felt her hands tied and glared at Longarm.

122

"You bastard! It was all a trick. There isn't any train, is there? Probably no avalanche either. What a fool I've been. You probably have the gems."

"You didn't tell me where they were. You carry all of them or half?"

"He has half of the beauties. Carries them on him all the time. Doesn't trust anyone, especially me. So what happens next, now that you're in control?"

"We wait for the train and I deal with Eric."

"He's not as easy as he looks," Riane said. "I'm betting on Eric."

Toby locked the door with an inside bolt. It was the only entrance to the telegraph office.

"You have a rifle in here?" Longarm asked. Toby shook his head.

"Then I have to go out there and get Eric before he gets cold and tries to come back in here." Longarm had finished wrapping up his wounded arm. He had his shirt in place, his jacket on, and his overcoat buttoned up. He checked his six-gun to be sure it had five shots. He took another round from his belt and loaded it into the empty chamber, then eased the hammer down on the live one.

Toby came over by the door and spoke softly so Riane couldn't hear.

"You know there isn't a snowslide or a rescue train. But my call for help did stir up the folks at the Union Pacific junction. They're sending in old engine 437 and one car with the county sheriff and six deputies. We should have some help here within half an hour."

Longarm nodded. "Now all I have to do is capture Heinrich before he gets so cold he wants to come inside." He looked out the window in the door but couldn't see the robber. He handed Toby Riane's six-gun.

"You know how to use that?"

"Yes, sir."

"Use it if you have to. Just don't let her get free. I'm counting on you." Longarm slipped outside into the below-freezing weather. There was a hint of more snow in the air. He moved with caution to the left for a better view of the platform and the tracks.

Heinrich hunched against three baggage carts lined up on the platform. Two were loaded with some kind of freight awaiting the morning train. They cut the wind for Heinrich.

Longarm saw how he could get closer, within revolver range of the man. He would run around the back side of the station house and come up just beyond the baggage carts.

His joints felt cold and stiff as he tried to run. It turned into a kind of jog for a few steps, and then his knees began to work, and he hurried around the station and up the far end. He came around the building and checked the baggage carts.

Heinrich still huddled there. Longarm walked forward, his handgun in front of him at arm's length, zeroing in on the robber. At twenty feet, Longarm bellowed a command.

"Don't move, Heinrich, or you're breakfast for some lucky buzzard."

Heinrich looked up and snorted. "Figured you'd be here sooner or later. Got a surprise for you. His arms had been folded, and Longarm saw the puff of fire as the man's handgun shot from under his arm. The slug whined close to Longarm, and he jolted to the right at the sound. Then he fired.

His round would have been dead center, but as he squeezed the trigger, Heinrich lunged to the side and ran across the tracks into the snow and the deep woods.

Longarm heard a train whistle to the north. Should he follow Heinrich or make sure he had one of them and get Riane on the train and in proper handcuffs and on the way to jail?

He chose Heinrich. With any good luck he'd have him caught and be back before the train could move out. He ran for the woods with only two seconds lost in the mind exercises.

The woods began just beyond the tracks, and Longarm plowed through the snow, following Heinrich's tracks to the trees, then stepping into the sifted snow that covered the ground in the woods with less than three or four inches. It was enough to track a man in during daylight, but not in the dark.

Longarm tried, then stopped and listened. He heard nothing. He didn't have the slightest idea in which direction to go. The snow was crisp and made a crunching and cracking sound when he walked. Then why wasn't he hearing any movement by Heinrich?

124

Probably because the robber had hunkered down somewhere waiting.

After two or three minutes of silence, Longarm charged straight ahead thirty yards into the woods, to a large pine tree, and stopped behind it. He heard no reaction from Heinrich. How did this city man get so good in the snow-covered woods all of a sudden? Longarm turned at right angles and ran for twenty yards, then stopped.

He thought he heard one step somewhere to his right. Then he could hear nothing but the train as it rumbled into the station. It was one engine and a single passenger car, and he heard the rig slow and stop.

He was in a slightly less dense section of the woods, and the moonlight gave him a better view of the area. Fewer trees, almost no brush. He looked for a dark blob that shouldn't have been there. Something, anything. some crunching to the left. He whirled just in time to see a big possum drop from a tree and scutter away behind a pine.

Where was Heinrich?

He heard voices and shouts over at the station. Toby would take care of things and hold them until he got back. But where was Heinrich? Longarm checked for tracks now that he could see better, with more moonlight coming through the trees. He made an arc searching for those footprints. He came to the edge of the woods fifty yards past the station but found nothing. He went forward twenty yards and made another arc around the spot where Heinrich had run into the woods.

He was at the deepest part of the arc when he heard the train hiss steam as the brakes came off, then the screech of steel on steel as the drive wheels spun on the rails before they gained traction. The train was leaving!

What had happened? He turned and ran flat-out for the tracks. When he arrived two minutes later, he saw the engine backing rapidly away to the north. Someone ran toward him from the end of the station house.

"Halt. Who the hell are you?"

"I'm U.S. Deputy Marshal Long. Who are you?"

"Deputy County Sheriff Ihander. What the hell is happening here?"

"You tell me. Did your sheriff take the woman prisoner back north?"

"Not that I know of. A woman met us and said the two robbers had escaped into town. One was wounded, and they were trying to find the doctor. Three of us chased that way; then five minutes later we heard the train start up."

Longarm swore silently as he ran to the telegrapher's office. The door was shut and the lights off. On the other side of the unlocked door, he found Toby behind the counter, tied hand and foot and gagged. Longarm tore off the gag.

"What happened?"

"Oh, damn, Marshal. I really failed you. How could I miss with the robber tied up and a woman to boot?"

"How did you?"

"Just after you left, she pleaded with me to untie her ankles. Said she had to go to the outhouse. She said I was a gentleman and I could wait outside, but she simply had to go or she'd foul herself.

"I took her. She went in, and before I knew it, she smashed the door open, dumping me in the snowbank. She jumped on me like a wild woman, bashed my head with a rock, and got the gun you left me and marched me back here."

Longarm untied Toby's hands and feet and toasted himself at the fire. He threw three more chunks of wood on the blaze.

"Not your fault, Toby. I just wanted both of them. I should have settled for half of them and half the jewels right now and worked at getting Heinrich later."

"He's with the girl. Heinrich said he tricked you. When he came back, he said he went into the woods only ten yards and let you run past him, then came back here. They must have used their gun on the engineer and made him back the train out of the station."

"Can they go far that way?"

"Sure, they can back up all the way to the junction."

Longarm took a long breath and let it out slowly so he wouldn't scream in rage. That pair was continuing to be as slippery as a polecat on a greased log at high noon in July.

He checked his watch. It showed a little after four A.M. They had five hours until the train got in from Salt Lake. By that

126

time Riane and friend could be on a westbound heading for San Francisco.

"Make sure the northbound stops here," Longarm said. "These deputy sheriffs and me all want a ride out to the Union Pacific. Until then, I'm going to have a nap on your bunk over there."

He couldn't sleep. The robbers were still free. He got up and examined the box on the high shelf. The jewels were still there.

Toby grinned. "At least I did that part right. She didn't even look in her valise. Before she got the gun, I put some nails from my repair drawer in her bag when she wasn't looking. Figured it was about the same weight as all those diamonds.

"She hefted the valise but never looked inside. Then the train came, and she didn't have time to do much but tie me up and blow out the lamp and get out and lie her way onto the train. She sent the deputies running for town in a rush."

"You done good, Toby. Don't worry about the rest of it. We'll get her yet. Now we have half the jewels back. That's what I'd call a good day's work."

Longarm settled down on the small bunk, and a moment later went to sleep.

Chapter 14

What a great way to wake up. Longarm felt something brush his cheek, and he made a weak wave with one hand to scare it away. It came back, and this time he roused enough to see a mass of dark brown hair spilling over his face and to feel lips hard against his.

Soft hands touched his face, and his eyes came fully open.

"Kimberly," he whispered. "About time you got here. Is the train out there?"

She laughed and caught his hand and helped him stand from the low bunk.

"It is and waiting for you. Let's hurry."

He took the small cardboard box down from the top shelf, checked to be sure the gems were still there, and shook hands with Toby. "You do good work. I'll get a letter of thanks sent to you."

Less than a half hour later the morning train from Salt Lake City pulled into the station at Junction and the main tracks to the coast. They would have a two-hour wait for the next westbound.

Longarm talked to the station agent, a man with curly blond hair, a waxed mustache, and penetrating blue eyes. At sixty years of age, he still had pink cheeks and a sparkle in his eye and couldn't stop staring at Kimberly.

"My, but you are a pretty one," the agent said. "I can say that at my age and not get slapped. My, my, my. What a beauty." He shook his head and turned back to Longarm.

"You want to know about the two young people who commandeered our help train sent down to Deweyville?"

"Yes, sir. The blond girl and the nearly six foot man. What happened to them?"

"Not sure," the station agent said. "The engine coming back was a big surprise to us. By the time they got it switched into our yard here, the pair had jumped off and vanished. Before we had a chance to take a good look for them, the nine-thirty-five westbound came in, and we had the usual questions and confusions. People think this is the Salt Lake City station, so we have a lot of answers to give. One man wouldn't believe he wasn't already in Salt Lake City.

"When the nine-thirty-five whistled out of here, we couldn't find that little blond-haired cutie anywhere. Chances are they both slipped onto that westbound and we didn't see them."

"I'm afraid you're right about that. When's the next train heading west?"

"Four-thirty-two this afternoon."

"That gives them a seven-hour head start."

"Best we can do. Oh, there's a work train coming through here at noon, but it has to hit a siding down the tracks a ways to clear the eastbound. Not sure if it would beat the regular train into Elko or not."

"We'll wait," Longarm decided. They looked outside and saw only two houses and a pretense of a hotel. The station boasted a small coffee shop for passengers, so they turned in there, put down their bags, and had sandwiches and coffee.

Longarm stashed the small cardboard box of gems in his traveling bag without telling Kimberly. No use taking any chances. She didn't ask about it. She had sent a telegram to the Junction to watch for the two robbers, but it had done no good.

Now they waited.

The warmth of the small eatery made them forget the cold outside. He checked his two minor wounds in his shoulder and arm, applied some healing salve from the emergency supplies he carried in his bag, and then they continued to wait.

Kimberly looked at the route map provided by the Union Pacific and the Central Pacific.

"Looks like there would be no practical place for them to stop before Sacramento," she said. "Elko is just a little place, and there isn't much else across Nevada and into Sacramento."

"What about Reno?"

She twisted her mouth thinking about it. "My guess would be that it isn't big enough. Anyway, by now they must be getting anxious to get to where they're going. You said you figured they were heading somewhere and not just running to cash in the stones one at a time."

"Agreed," Longarm said. He looked at the map, which was marked with Central Pacific from the junction area on west. "I'd say Sacramento should be our next stop. No chief marshal there. He's located in San Francisco for the northern California district. I've worked with him before."

Longarm went to the telegraph office and sent two wires. One went to the county sheriff at Sacramento, and the other one to Chief U.S. Marshal Penrod Rudolph in San Francisco. He told them both the same thing, updating them on the chase, the time the fugitives left the junction, and the expected destination.

He asked the San Francisco marshal if he had any record of any kind of a Chinese connection for any type of smuggling in and out of California. Riane had mentioned China two or three times in their conversations, and it made him curious. A Chinese connection for the gem robbers would make sense. The stolen Chicago gems could be smuggled into China and sold there with no trouble from the officials.

Just before their train left, Longarm received a reply from Marshal Rudolph in San Francisco. He opened the envelope and read:

"Longarm, Junction Station, Utah. Have been following your chase of two Chicago robbers. Strongly suspect they are coming here to sell the gems to some international smuggler. Strong chance that China may be involved. Now watching two suspects. Advise soonest of your arrival, any update on Chicago robbers. Signed, U.S. Marshal P. Rudolph."

He showed the wire to Kimberly. "No stop for us at Sacramento as we'd talked about. We're going straight through to San Francisco."

She kissed him. "I've always wanted to see San Francisco."

They saw it a little over two days later.

The weather: fifty-five degrees and threatening to rain. The natives were chilled. Longarm carried his overcoat and figured it must be spring. Kimberly wanted to go swimming in the Pacific Ocean. Longarm talked her out of it.

They arrived about four in the afternoon and took one room at a hotel. Then Longarm hustled over to the Federal Building to talk with Marshal Rudolph.

The U.S. marshal for the northern California district was a large man, with bushy eyebrows and lots of dark brown hair that had three cowlicks in it and refused to lie in any one direction for very long without a lot of hair grease to hold it in place. He refused to use it.

Chief Rudolph wore spectacles, claiming nearsightedness. The half-glasses perched on the end of a nose that had been broken more than once and failed to heal straight. Deep green eyes stared at Longarm over the horn-rimmed half-specs.

Longarm handed the chief marshal the six-inch-square cardboard box and let him open it.

"Gawddamn! I'll be gawddamned to hell. These all real? Is this all of them?"

"Half, if I can believe Riane Moseley. She said the other half were always in the possession of Eric Heinrich, proving that he trusted no one, not even her."

"A falling out of thieves?"

"No, sir, just a healthy respect for man's distrust of others and recognition of the power of greed."

"I understand. Do you know how many individual stones are here?"

"No idea."

The marshal picked up a telephone on his desk and instructed someone to report to his office at once. Longarm had seen telephones before, but never used one much. A true marvel of the modern age.

The man who came in was small and hunched over, and wore a white shirt and tie but no jacket. He carried a jeweler's loupe in his hand.

"You have something?" he asked.

The marshal pointed to the box, and the small man's eyes widened.

"The three of us will sort out, categorize, and record each of these stones, and you will place an estimated value on each one. Then they and your evaluation of them will be sealed, and the three of us will sign the receipt, and they will be held in our safe for the Chicago police to sign off when we deliver them to their representative. I'll wire the Chicago police to send a bonded messenger as soon as we're finished."

It took them until one A.M. to do all of the cataloging and evaluating. All three men were tired. Longarm and the marshal had talked silently to one side as the jeweler did his work.

By one o'clock, Longarm knew there was a connection there in San Francisco between the jewel robbers and a man known for his expertise in smuggling, both in and out of the United States.

"We've been watching him for the past two weeks. We know everywhere he goes, who he talks to, what he does during the day and the night. We know more about him than his mother or either of his two mistresses."

"What's his name, and when can I go along with your man?" Longarm asked.

"Tomorrow morning you'll meet our man. His name is Seth Talbot. Good deputy, been with me five years. Knows the inside of this town like nobody else. Speaks enough Mandarin Chinese to get by. Seth says that his target seems to be getting ready for some kind of a big shipment. We don't know if it's coming in or going out of the country. Somehow the stolen gems from Chicago figure into the plot."

"Even half of them?"

"Half is better than no loot at all. We're not sure if the two who pulled the job were the only ones involved on the Chicago end of the robbery. Seems like a lot of coincidences happened to let two newcomers to the jewel robbery business get away with so much loot."

"That's worried me some, too. But if Chicago has a hand in it, I saw no one tailing the robbers or trying to protect them."

"That's the one element that doesn't seem to fit. Let's talk about it again in the morning. Now we sign off on these gems,

132

make sure our jeweler is clean, and lock up everything in the safe, all signed, sealed tight, and put to rest."

They did.

Longarm got into the room a little after two A.M. Kimberly slept under a sheet and a blanket. As he undressed, she sat up, rubbing her eyes.

"I just had the most wonderful dream about you," she said, the hint of a laugh in her words. Then the same hint slipped into her smile.

"How good was it?"

"Four times fantastic as I remember, once a way we've never done before." She let the sheet fall and he saw she was naked. She'd been waiting for him.

He stripped and slid in beside her. Kimberly moved on top of him and kissed his lips hungrily.

"Oh, damn but this is going to be good. I've been waiting almost three days to get you bare-assed and in my bed again."

Longarm held her away. "You mean you don't want to put on a fancy dress and go to the famous San Francisco Opera with all of the swells?"

She wriggled between his arms and kissed him, and one hand found his crotch, where there was already the start of a long, hard pole.

"Sweet darling. The opera was over three hours ago. Maybe tomorrow night we'll go to the opera. Tonight San Francisco is for making love."

"What a great way to end the day." He found her breast with his hand and caressed it gently, rounding it and rounding it and then tweaking her pulsating nipple. Kimberly moaned. He felt his penis fill with hot blood and harden, pushing against her thigh. Slowly he ground its length against her, and she moved so it centered between her legs and pressed against her silken thatch.

"My goodness, Mr. Long. I do believe that you are becoming just the least little bit interested in my naked, hot, and wanting body."

"Me?" He reached over and kissed one of her breasts a dozen times in the rounding pattern, then kissed her surging nipple, and she cried out in wonder and frustration. Gently Longarm nibbled her nipple, then bit it harder, and she yelped in pain and desire.

Her hand caught his tool, and she pumped it.

"Do that about ten more times, and you'll have a handful," he said.

Kimberly grinned and threw back the light cover, sitting cross-legged at his hip and pumping with her right hand on his long, purple-tipped tool.

She bent and kissed the arrow head of him, then licked it, all the time pumping him with her hand.

Longarm leaned back on his arms, his body almost in a sitting position as he watched her. His hips felt the pressure, and now they began a slow little dance, meeting the downward strokes of her hand.

"You've done this before, Kimberly. You're not a virgin after all."

"Fooled you for a while." She licked her lips. "Fact is I pumped off the first boy I was ever with. I was sixteen and we went swimming, and when we got tired, we lay on the bank on a blanket.

"He said he wanted to see my breasts all bare. Said he'd never seen a girl's bare tits. I wanted to see him, too, so I pulled down the top of my swimming suit. He stared and then touched me, and I stopped him and said he had to show himself to me.

"He didn't hesitate; just pulled off his pants and there he was, stiff and hot and ready. He touched my breasts and fondled them. So I touched him and played with him. He showed me how to pump, and after four strokes he shot his cum all over my leg.

"I was surprised how worked up he got and how he panted and grunted and yelped when he came. He kept playing with me, and before he even asked me, I took off the rest of my suit. I was so hot and curious, I'd have done anything right then.

"He explored my body, and I did the same with him, and in ten minutes he was hot and ready again. We made love five times that afternoon in an hour and a half. He just couldn't get enough. Finally the sun went down and we dressed and ran for home."

"That was your very first time?"

"My first five times," she said and grinned, remembering. Then she pumped harder, kissed his arrow point, and a moment later

134

Longarm couldn't hold it anymore. His hips pounded upward, and she yelped when a spurt of cum shot out of him and narrowly missed her face.

"My god, is that what happens inside me?" she asked. He pumped six more times and shot another six loads into the air. Then she lay on him, her hips pounding hard, and before he knew it, she tore into a climax of her own, crying out a dozen times with little animal noises that surprised and thrilled Longarm. She lay there, her slender body trembling and shaking as spasm after spasm drilled through it.

Then she was through, and she collapsed on him, and they both rested.

Later Kimberly lifted away from him, lay on her side, and propped her head up with her hand.

"That was different—not as good, but educational. I still miss your big rod inside me, just plunging and poking up a storm!"

"I miss that, too, but give me a few minutes. Neither one of us is sixteen anymore."

Kimberly laughed. Her eyes pinched a moment, and a sigh escaped her lips. She watched him with a touch of a frown. "Longarm, I don't feel like I'm helping you much on the jewel robbery. I mean, I said we would work as a team, and it seems like I don't do much, besides keep your bed warm and your great body satisfied. I should be investigating more."

"You've helped a lot. I told you I like to work alone. I haven't let you do much. Besides, I don't want you to get killed. You've taken more chances now than you should."

She snuggled closer. "Now I feel better." She pushed back to look at him. "You didn't say, but I'd guess you found half of the jewels, the ones Riane had."

"Right, that's what was in that box in the telegrapher's office. If you didn't know about them, nobody could make you tell if I had them or not."

"Oh, great, so they would have tortured me to death thinking I was lying to them."

"Wouldn't have happened. Anyway, half of the stolen jewels are in a safe place. They have been checked, recorded, analyzed, and evaluated, and signed off by me, Chief Marshal Rudolph, and a professional jeweler. They're awaiting a personal guard from the Chicago police department to pick them up."

"Good. Job half done."

"And I'll send a wire to your firm telling them that you assisted in retrieving the gems and that I certify the recovery and that you deserve your commission."

She kissed him. "I knew you were wonderful, in and out of bed. This proves it. Now, a surprise. I want to try something different."

"Different like what? Two men at once?"

"No, silly, how could I make love to two . . ." Her brows went up and she giggled. "No, not a chance. Here, let me show you what I mean."

She jumped off the bed and spread her legs two feet apart on the wooden floor. Then she looked at him. "Isn't it great being able to make love and not freeze ourselves to pieces?"

"It sure is." Longarm watched the lovely girl standing there as naked as a newborn babe but a thousand times more exciting. "What's this new thing?"

She bent and grabbed her ankles with her hands. She stood, nodded to herself, and then turned with her back to him and grabbed her ankles again. She looked at him upside down from between her legs.

"See anything that looks interesting?"

Longarm chuckled. "I see a beautiful round little bottom with two pink holes."

"Try either one you want," Kimberly said. "Right now. I don't know how long I can stand on my head this way."

Longarm stood and eased up to her. He caught the crease between stomach and legs with his hands to hold her and angled forward. He chose the lower spot, all moist and outer lips spread and pink, wanting.

He eased forward, and she yelped in wonder, then moaned as he pressed deeply into her at a slightly different angle than usual. The pressure on him was more intense as well.

"Do me, Longarm. Screw me hard and fast!"

He plunged forward, his hands holding her to him, and soon the two bodies worked together. He heard her shout something, and he held her from falling, pounding like a steam ram into her. She couldn't move; he held her fast and the pressure built. Soon he felt her shuddering into her climax, but by then he was too far gone himself, and he gave a strangled cry of victory and success as he blasted his seed deep into her waiting vagina. With the last stroke they almost fell down, but he grabbed her hips and pulled back and kept them both standing.

Kimberly lowered her head, still panting, her neck and chest splotched with the red of her climax, and looked up at him from between her legs.

"Longarm, what the hell do we do now?"

He hadn't even had time to recover when she said it, and the total humor of it hit him like a locomotive blasting into a six-hundred-pound steer on a high-speed run. He came away from her and fell on the bed, screeching with laughter. She lay beside him, staring quizzically at his behavior.

"Think about it," he said. "There we were in this ungodly position, and we've both just climaxed, and you ask what the hell do we do now?"

"Fall down, I guess." She guffawed, and that caused him to roar again, and soon they were laughing so hard tears streamed down their cheeks and they clung to each other for support on the bed.

He pulled the light covers over them, and they snuggled together, still laughing. Longarm had only a fleeting few seconds to think about the next day. The China connection. Riane Moseley had been serious when she mentioned China. Now he was anxious to get started.

Only moments after the laughter had died away, he and Kimberly went to sleep in each other's arms.

Chapter 15

Seth Talbot stood slim and tall, a slow grin coming out of a lean face with narrow eyes, a big nose, and topping it all, close-cropped black hair. Longarm had known him for five minutes, and he liked the man immediately. Nothing fake or phoney. What you saw was Seth Talbot and no mistake.

They sat in an outer office at the Federal Building, going over what Seth knew about the Chinese connection in San Francisco and how it might tie in with the Chicago gem robbery.

"Can't say for sure now," Seth admonished. "Looks like it could be. I been working on this one for two months, and something is going to happen soon."

"You said this Chop Soo runs an import firm bringing in mostly goods from China?"

"Right. Chop Soo has been around Chinatown for years. He must be well over eighty. Moves like he's twenty, slender, wears the long braid, always dresses in Chinese style. He runs Chinatown and thirty thousand or so Chinamen. He's rarely seen outside of his little kingdom anymore, down on Van Knowlen Street. He has layers of protection up to three blocks away, and it gets thicker and tougher as you work toward his palace.

"He has men he calls 'ministers' who do the outside contact work for him, all the way from city hall to the smallest Chinese merchant selling goods in Chinatown. He's the dominant force to deal with down there."

"Opium?"

"Mostly. Supplies all of the pleasure palaces and opium dens in San Francisco. Lately he's been bringing in some heroin, too, but we can't quite get our finger on the right ship. It all comes in through the harbor. We beef up our watch, but still the stuff gets through, almost all of it.

"Not that opium and heroin are illegal. No law against buying, selling, or using any form of drugs in this country or the state of California. But the federals do impose a good-size import duty on them, and this is why they're smuggled."

"How do the gems tie in?"

"That's the tough part. A white man we think is from Chicago has been talking to some of the 'ministers' straight from Chop Soo. In teahouses, in some of the best restaurants in town, in fancy buggies. One of the 'ministers' we've identified is Chang Toy. He has a police record going back ten years. Arrests for all kind of crimes, but no convictions. Best lawyers Chinese money could buy, all white lawyers. For five years he's been clean.

"Now he's highly respected and feared in the Chinese district. When he talks, everyone stops and listens. He cuts a wide swath, and we're not sure why, except that he usually speaks for Chop Soo."

"Does he speak English?"

"Yes, as good as we do and that's one good point. Most of Chop Soo's people don't. This one does and makes a lot of contacts for his boss outside of Chinatown. He works the docks as well. The dock workers are all white guys. They have a union going down there and have the work all tied up tight. But this Chang Toy seems to get along with everyone. My guess is that he spreads around a lot of greenbacks to pave the way.

"A Chinese ship from Canton docks tomorrow. It came into the bay yesterday and is anchored for another day, until the dock it wants is clear. We've seen Chang Toy in that area on Pier 13 twice in the last two days. He usually talks with a gang boss there, a white man called Hook Younger."

"You have any help on this?"

139

"Another deputy, Unruh, has been lending a hand. Now he's full-time with us. He'll be in shortly, and we'll see what we can plan out. I want to keep a tail on Chang Toy. There's a hotel near Chinatown that Chang uses for visiting whites now and then. We'll stake it out as well and pass a few greenbacks to the hotel clerk to watch for your Chicago couple."

"They could have been in town a day already, if we guessed right," Longarm said. "I want to work the hotel. I know the pair."

Seth held up a finger. "Remember, we don't want you to arrest them on sight. The whole ploy now is to use them as bait and see if we can nail at least Chang Toy and maybe Chop Soo at the same time. We could get them for receiving stolen goods, maybe tie them in with the shipment from China if it's illegal or smuggled."

"Those aren't my instructions," Longarm said. "My specific orders are to capture the two robbers and the jewels and facilitate the return of both to Chicago. I'll need some new palaver from your chief marshal to change my job."

Seth grinned. He scratched his head a moment and then nodded. "Yep, I agree. I'd do the same thing in your place. Let's go in and see Marshal Rudolph."

It took five minutes, and Longarm was released from his previous orders and given new ones. On a cooperative chase like this one the resident U.S. marshal had control of any other marshals working in his district. Longarm would work closely with Deputy U.S. Marshal Seth Talbot and take his orders through him.

They waited another half hour for Unruh to show up; then when he didn't, they took a hack across most of San Francisco to the waterfront area and stopped at a small hotel a block from the docks. It was called the Carlton and had seen better days. The outside looked shabby, but inside it was bright and clean. The two of them talked to the manager, then to the hotel clerk.

"They could be traveling alone or together," Longarm told the clerk. "They might take one room or two. The important idea is if and when they arrive, you notify us immediately. Have you seen them arrive in the past two days?"

The clerk shook his head.

"Do you know if they're now living here?"

"Can't say for sure, sir. I don't see all of the people on my shift. Some come late and leave early—"

"This pair will be here for several days, I'd expect," Seth cut in. "Watch for them. You heard your manager's instructions."

The clerk, a rotund, short man with a mustache and a vanishing chin, nodded and agreed to be alert and to notify the U.S. marshal's office if he saw the couple. The two deputies left.

Today Longarm wore his tweed frock coat, brown town pants, flannel shirt, and a brown calfskin vest. His stovepipe cavalry boots were black, and under his frock coat he carried his Colt .44–40 in a black leather cross-draw rig. His brown wide-brimmed hat had a flat crown.

Seth, who had on a black suit, white shirt, black vest, and a derby hat, shrugged as he looked at Longarm outside. "I guess you won't stand out too much in that outfit. The hat would do it if nothing does. Don't want this pair to spot you and get scared off."

"No chance," Longarm said. "When I'm inside I won't wear the hat and I'll stay well back out of sight."

Seth nodded. "I shouldn't be trying to tell you how to do your work. I've heard about you for years. Glad to finally work with you. Well, I've got to check on our friend Chang Toy. About this time most days he holds court at a little Chinese restaurant where half the customers are Chinese and the rest whites. Makes it easy for him to cross over and talk with the white devils."

"You said something about a ship coming in. Today or tomorrow?"

"I checked with the dockmaster. That space opens up at ten o'clock tomorrow morning. We'll have a dozen men there if we can get them, also some San Francisco police."

Longarm looked at the hotel. He had a feeling that Riane and her tall friend were staying in the place. They'd had plenty of time if they'd come straight through.

Seth waved. "I'll see you tonight at the office about six. We can have dinner and compare what we found out."

Longarm nodded and went back into the hotel. He thought of food and looked at the dining room. It was not the hotel's best feature. He walked to the door and looked over the eatery, then stepped up to the desk at the side of the entrance. A woman

141

cashier sat there, near a man with a pad ready to make a list or take reservations.

"Do you have room service?" Longarm asked the man, who wore a shabby tuxedo and gloves that at one time had been white.

"But of course," he said. He had a slight French accent, mostly by imitation, Longarm decided.

"For a one-dollar service fee we will bring you anything on the menu at the usual menu price of course."

"Has a small blond lady with short hair and a great smile ordered anything sent to her room?"

The man frowned for a moment. "Yes, yes. Yesterday, just before the dinner rush. Two dinners and a bottle of wine. It was an excellent choice."

"Is she in the dining room now?" Longarm asked.

"But no. She said she didn't like big crowds. Pretty girl."

"What room did you send the dinner to?"

"But I cannot tell you that."

Longarm took out his badge and his identification. The man stared at it for a moment and shrugged.

"All right, it was room 310. I remember. I fancied going up there myself to deliver the food. She was, how do you say it, a delicious bit of fluff."

"Indeed she is. Thanks. Don't tell anyone I asked you about her. Understand?"

The head waiter nodded and moved toward the entrance, where a couple had come in for an early lunch.

Longarm ordered a bottle of wine from the cashier and had her put it in a paper sack. He took it into the lobby. He checked to be sure neither of the two robbers was there. Then he found a bellboy and told him exactly what he wanted him to do. A dollar tip brought a promise to deliver the bottle of wine to room 310 in precisely fifteen minutes.

Longarm walked up the stairs to the third floor and past room 310. He listened at room 313, across the hall and one door down from 310. No one seemed to be inside. He knocked softly and no one came. Longarm used his bent-wire skeleton key and opened the door easily. Inside he could see that the room was not occupied.

He settled down to wait. By opening the door a half inch, he could look directly at the door of room 310.

The bellboy was two minutes early. He knocked on the door, and when it opened, Longarm saw the flash of short blond hair and then Riane Moseley's face as she laughed and reached out for the wine.

"Yes, that's the kind of thing he would do," she said. She waved at the bellboy, who turned and walked away. She peered after him, then took a short step into the hall and checked both ways. When she saw no one watching or lurking, she shrugged and went back into her room and closed the door.

Longarm grinned. He had her! No, he didn't. He couldn't wade in there and arrest her and Eric Heinrich even if he was with her. He had new orders. The damn China connection. He left the room, didn't bother to lock it, and went down the steps to the lobby. He stood there a minute. A thick, heavy fog oozed along the street outside. A man could get lost in that.

Longarm waited a few minutes, then left the hotel and tried to walk back to the Federal Building. In ten minutes he was lost. He hailed a hack and rode the rest of the way. He had been heading in the wrong direction.

On the second floor, he walked into the U.S. marshal's office and wondered why no one sat at the front desk. The door was open into the chief marshal's room, and he went to it and knocked gently.

The dark-haired woman secretary who had been at the desk near the door rushed out, her hands covering her face, great sobs shaking her body. Longarm started to stop her; then he stepped into U.S. Marshal Rudolph's office.

The large man stood looking out the window into the sea of fog that still covered the street. Rudolph turned, his face worried, angry. A hint of relief cracked the strain for a moment; then the anger came back.

"Thank God you're all right. You haven't heard about Seth. Somebody just killed him in a Chinese restaurant uptown. Put a long knife through his side and into his heart. He evidently died without making a sound."

The chief marshal turned back to the window, and a tear edged out of his eye and rolled down his cheek.

143

"Chang Toy?" Longarm asked. "You want me to go up there?"

"No!" The word came with explosive force. Rudolph turned, his eyes closed, his face still working. One big hand scrubbed down across his eyes and his cheek, and he shook his head.

"No, Longarm, you stay here. I've lost one man today. I don't want to lose another one. It couldn't have been Toy directly. He was across the room with a city councilman and four other Anglos. Nobody saw anyone go near Seth. But someone did.

"No one in the Chinese community will even talk with the police. It's like a man was murdered with a hundred people watching, but nobody saw a thing."

"Toy and Chop Soo must be worried about the progress Seth was making against them," Longarm said. "I found the Chicago girl in the Carlton Hotel. I saw her, identified her. The man is probably there as well. I didn't know what else to do. This is foreign land for me."

Rudolph looked out the window again, then with slow steps walked back to his big desk and sat behind it. He shook his head again, blew his nose on a big white handkerchief, and wiped his eyes.

When he looked up, he was back to business. "Did you meet Olaf Unruh? He's been working with Seth on this one. He was mostly watching the pier. He at least knows the territory. How would Toy know that Seth would be there this noon? Seth didn't decide to go until shortly before you came this morning."

"It must have been set up by Chang Toy," Longarm said. "You want me to go bring him in for questioning?"

"The police have already talked to him and about forty others who were in the restaurant. They released everyone."

"The hired help?"

"All from the old country. I'd wager not a one except the waiters can speak any English except hello, good-bye, and thank you."

"Chang Toy must be worried, or he wouldn't take out one of your men so close to the delivery."

"Don't try to see Chang Toy," Rudolph ordered. "He has a big house in the Chinese section, but you couldn't get within two blocks of it before he'd know you were coming, and he'd

144

be a mile away before you rang his bell. Forget about going to see him in Chinatown."

"What about Chop Soo?"

"How can we involve him? No direct connection to Chang Toy. Not on record. Everyone knows he works for Soo, but nobody would admit it."

"Maybe one of them will contact the Chicago twins. You want me to watch their room?"

"Best idea so far. You keep them under tabs, and Unruh can check on the pier. Always a chance that dock will clear early and that the damn ship will pull in early and be half-unloaded before we know it's dropped anchor."

"I'll watch the room. We might get lucky. Otherwise we'll work the ship. The girl said something about going to China. I'm not sure if she was joking or not."

"Oh, this Chop Soo, he's an importer. He brings in thousands of tons of goods from China every month. He's a master smuggler. I don't know how we can spot any opium coming in or jewels going out, even if we watch every box and bundle as it's unloaded."

"We'll worry that when it happens. I better get back to the hotel."

Longarm took a cab to the Carlton Hotel. He ordered two big sandwiches and two bottles of cold beer from the dining room and carried them upstairs to room 313. The deputy U.S. marshal wedged some folded paper under the door to keep it cracked open a half inch, sat in the straight-backed chair, and had his lunch. He wondered what Kimberly was doing. Probably shopping.

Two o'clock came and passed. At three a waiter brought a tray of food and stopped in front of room 310. Longarm saw two meals on plates. Evidently Eric was in the room as well.

They set the dishes outside about 3:30. A short time later, two small men came up the hall and stopped in front of the door at 310. Both were Chinese. Longarm loosened his six-gun.

They knocked, and when the door opened, one of them handed an envelope to Riane, who left the door ajar as she read the message.

She opened the door wider and nodded. "Yes, this would be a good time. We'll be right with you." She closed the door and a moment later came out wearing a hair-concealing hat and an overcoat and carrying her red reticule. Eric Heinrich, looking grumpy and not at all pleased, came out behind her. He locked the door, and the two Chinese led the way down the hall.

Just before he went down the steps, Heinrich turned and looked along the empty hall behind him. After pausing a moment, he vanished down the stairs.

Longarm eased out of the room and followed them. He almost lost them in the street. They walked toward the docks. At least the fog had burned away, and the sun was trying to poke its way through a scattering of clouds. He saw a thermometer on a building that showed it was fifty-five degrees. Longarm felt as if it were spring, not December.

The four ahead of him crossed the street. He hung on the other side and kept up with them. Twice Heinrich looked back. He wore his cold-weather overcoat and looked out of place. He was checking to see if someone was following them.

Longarm hung back, stared into a window display of some new men's clothes, then moved on. The four people turned abruptly into a storefront. Longarm could see no name on it as he approached. He crossed the street, and when he was within three feet of the door, he realized that it had no outside handle. It had to be opened from the inside.

He paused at the curb, watching the fancy carriages moving up and down the street. When he turned back, he scrutinized the door again and the building in back of it. There was no building there at all, only what looked like it could be a staircase built between two large structures. Both were four stories tall and made of wood.

Longarm walked on down the street, crossed to the other side, and went into a store. He stood near the front window and watched the door across the street, but no one came out of it, and he saw no one try to get inside. What in the world was it?

He hadn't noticed it before, but now he became aware that they had walked into the very edge of Chinatown. On one end of the block all stores and people were Chinese. On the other end of the block there were mostly Germans and a few Mexicans and the rest Anglos.

Longarm memorized the names of the stores on both sides of the mysterious door and walked back toward the Federal

Building. Again he was not sure how to find it, so he took a cab. At least this time he had been heading in the right direction.

Longarm was shown into the marshal's office. Another man sat there talking with the chief deputy. Rudolph looked up and nodded. He pointed at Longarm.

"Unruh, this is the man I told you about, Deputy Custis Long, usually known as Longarm. Longarm, this is Olaf Unruh." Unruh stood and shook hands with Longarm. The two nodded.

"Sit down, both of you. Looks like we have our hands full. Unruh just told me that the dock the Chinese always use down on Pier 13 is empty. The word is that the Chinese boat will tie up there in two hours and unloading will begin at once. Hope you had a good lunch because we're all going to be working tonight!"

Chapter 16

Longarm withdrew a shotgun from the weapons room and went with six other deputies in a carriage toward the docks. The San Francisco police would have twenty men there, too, all under the command of Chief Marshal Rudolph. It there were any shooting involved, the lawmen would have plenty of firepower.

Rudolph met the deputies and police a block from the docks. He grouped them around him in an alley.

"This isn't a shootout, men," he cautioned. "We're not even sure this is the ship they'll be bringing in their contraband on. There could be a cache of stolen and smuggled jewels on board. If so, we want to find them.

"We'll watch for any of Chop Soo's men or Chang Toy's cutthroat Chinese. If they're there, chances are this is the boat we want. We'll be hidden around the docks, ready to move if we need to. Three short blasts on a police whistle will be the signal to swarm the ship being unloaded. Hold everyone in place when you get there. They will be unloading onto wagons most likely. More instructions will be coming. Remember, stay hidden where you're placed until time to move."

Longarm grunted at Unruh. "Doesn't sound too hard so far. This Chop Soo must carry a lot of weight around here."

Unruh pushed a battered black hat back on his head and snorted. "Give him another ten years and he'll be running the

148

whole city. The guy is a brilliant a field general, and he knows how to control people. He's got over a thousand men working for him, I'm told."

They moved closer, each of the officers being placed within sight of the thirteenth pier and close to the empty berth where the Chinese ship was supposed to tie up.

Longarm and Unruh were positioned in a warehouse just across from the pier and within twenty-five yards of where the big hawsers would secure the Oriental ship. They sat down on some wooden boxes and waited. Darkness stole in when they didn't notice. A light fog blew in from the sea with the on-shore flow of air, but not thick enough to get lost in. It wafted and wavered, lifted a moment, came in heavier, but in another moment it cleared away.

"What exactly are we looking for?" Longarm asked.

Unruh pointed into the bay. A gray-painted, rusty oceangoing ship with steam power headed for the dock open on Pier 13.

"That's where the ship should dock," Unruh said. "Now we look for Chinese who are slipping around as if they aren't interested in the ship."

Longarm chuckled. Twenty men loafed around the dock. One man fished off the side. Half a dozen walked along as if they were visitors. A knot of Anglo men he figured were the longshoremen waited under a light. He could spot four Chinese even in the dark. Gas lights burned along the dock, giving off an eerie glow. How in the world would they be able to spot something illegal or that had not had the import duties paid?

Inspectors? Yes, there would be inspectors there to check the cargo.

"There, the third man down from the end of the dock. That's Chang Toy. I can tell by the cut of his suit. He's a flashy dresser. Wears nothing Chinese. He'll send a man with the first batch of goods. That will be the diversion. The next time he sends men with a shipment, we'll probably move in and stop it.

"We've tried that before, and come up with nothing but Chinese fans and bamboo furniture."

"What if the goods we want are in the first batch Chang Toy taps?" Longarm asked.

149

"Then we'll still get it, because we send two men to pick up that shipment after it leaves the dock area. They follow it, but don't let Chang Toy know."

"Ayuh . . . Sounds a little complicated to me. I'd rather know for sure who the bad guys are and go get them."

"It's different here, especially in and around Chinatown. But we'll manage."

They waited and watched the big ship nudged into the dock sideways with the help of some smaller pusher boats. When the craft had been tied securely to the dock, a gangplank came down and two San Francisco port officials went on board.

Soon workers on the steamer began to ready the ship for unloading. Hatches were removed. Goods piled up on the deck. After nearly an hour the papers were signed and the officials left the ship. Then the unloading started, with men carrying goods on their backs from the ship to the dockside. There were no fancy steam-powered cranes to do the work here as Longarm had seen at some ports.

"Watch the Chinese," Unruh said.

"Where's Chang Toy?"

"About where he was. Smoking a cigarette, watching the unloading."

Some of the goods went directly onto flat-bottomed wagons with no sides. When one was filled, it pulled away; then another took its place.

"There!" Unruh said. A small Chinese with a pigtail and in a Chinese long robe walked to a wagon and inspected some of the goods. He nodded and shouted at the driver, who left with the wagon only partly filled.

"Too obvious," Unruh said. "Wait."

Ten minutes later and four more departed wagons, another Chinese man went to a wagon and nodded at the driver. The rig was pulled by two white mules. The Chinese man left at once.

"Let's go," Unruh said. "This end is our baby." They ran across the street and toward the dock, then across it to where the wagon with two white mules had just started to move.

Longarm and Unruh tracked the rig for two blocks, then the Chinese they had seen at the docks jumped on board and began tearing at one of the boxes.

"Now!" Unruh barked. He and Longarm raced for the wagon. Longarm saw four policemen running at it from the other side. The Chinese man on the rig shouted at them, but they jumped on board the wagon and it stopped. The man in the robe chattered in Chinese, but none of the officers understood him.

At last he waved his hands to them and struggled with the words. "Mine. Own. Buy," he said. He lit a torch, lifted it high, and held up a piece of pottery, then a Chinese doll. From another box he'd opened he showed them fireworks made in China for the many Chinese festivals in Chinatown.

He went to each of the dozen boxes, opening them, showing the officers the goods. The deputies and police searched each box to its bottom and found nothing out of the ordinary or illegal, and no stolen jewels from the Orient.

The officers left the wagon and hurried back to the dock. Six more wagons had been lined up and were being examined by officers with torches.

Marshal Rudolph directed them. He had an angry expression on his face, and his fists were on his hips.

"What about that first wagon that Chang Toy sent off?" Longarm asked.

"Dammit, yes!" Marshal Rudolph yelped. "We sent Jones to trail along behind that one. Did he come back?"

No one had seen him.

Longarm and Unruh ran toward the street where they had seen that first wagon disappear. They hurried west on it for two blocks. Along the narrow passageway, Longarm stumbled over something at the side of a building. He went back and snapped a match with his thumb to get some light on the scene. It was a body.

Unruh checked the man's face.

"Damn, it's Jones. The too-obvious load was the one we should have followed. Where could there be any place around here that we could tie in with the smugglers?"

Longarm told Unruh about the mysterious door without an outside handle.

"Can you find it again?" Unruh asked.

They went back to the hotel, and Longarm oriented himself,

then walked quickly down the street to the door with the blank exterior.

"Seen these before," Unruh said. "Not a lot of them around. Usually the Chinese use them for private clubs."

"This was where they took the two Chicago Anglo jewel robbers," Longarm said.

Unruh stared at the other deputy a moment. "We better get back and tell the boss what happened. He likes to handle things like this."

Ten minutes later, the chief U.S. marshal for the northern California district listened to the two deputies tell him what had happened.

"We'd need a warrant to go through that private door," Marshal Rudolph said. "By the time we got the warrant, everyone in that whole damn block would be out of town somewhere, and we wouldn't learn a thing."

"I could quit the service and go in as a private citizen," Longarm said. "I wouldn't need a warrant then."

"Absolutely not. White men vanish in those Chinatown hovels and are never heard from again. You think I want Billy Vail screaming at me for the next twenty years if I lose you down there? We better just think on this overnight and see what we can come up with in the morning. We missed a shipment of jewels and probably a lot of unreported heroin and opium. So we'll get the next batch."

He slapped a riding crop against his leg. "I wish to hell I could do something. That makes two good men I've lost in the past twenty-four hours. There must be something damn big happening, and we don't even know what it is!"

They rode the carriage back to Longarm's hotel. He got out and paused.

"You want to come up for a drink? I've got a stash of good Maryland rye up there in case you're interested."

Marshal Rudolph shook his head. "Sounds tempting, but I can't come. Need to write a citation of bravery for Jones, the man who was murdered tonight. I need at least a couple of hours at the office yet. Sorry."

Longarm waved good-bye and hurried into the hotel and up to his and Kimberly's room. He knocked on the door. No answer.

Strange. He checked under the door but saw no light coming from the room. The door remained locked. He stood against the wall and reached over so he could turn the lock with his key and not expose himself to anyone firing from inside. Then he pushed the door hard, so it swung around and hit the wall. Nobody hiding behind it.

Longarm struck a match and held it inside the room as he crouched at the hall wall. No shot blasted at him. He heard no sound of any kind. He stood, peered around the door frame, saw no one, and stepped into the room.

It took a second match to get the lamp on the dresser lighted. No Kimberly. The bed had not been slept in; everything was in order. Then he saw the note on the dresser. He picked up the paper and read:

"Miss Kimberly Walkenhorst will be my guest for the next few days. If you wish to see her alive again, give up your hunt for the Chicago gems and return to Denver. When you get to Denver, the girl will be released."

No signature. The note had been carefully printed in block letters and written on a sheet of white paper folded in half.

Longarm found his Gladstone bag under the bed. He took out a spare box of rounds for his .44–40 and pushed it into his pocket. His loaded derringer lay safely in his vest. The knife was hidden in its usual spot in his right boot.

He blew out the lamp, stepped into the hall, locked the door, and hurried downstairs. Ten minutes later he ran up the steps to the Federal Building and inside the unguarded door. On the second floor he saw lights from under the U.S. marshal's office door and tried the handle, locked.

Longarm pounded on the door and waited. Chang Toy had kidnapped Kimberly, he knew for sure. How had Toy known about her? The man must have spies everywhere. Where could she be, and how could he get her back? Suddenly the assignment to find the jewels lost its urgency. First things first. Kimberly's life was much more important to him than all those jewels.

Quick footsteps sounded, moving toward the door, and then it swung open and Longarm stepped inside the U.S. marshal's office. He said nothing, only held out the note to the chief marshal.

Just before darkness fell, Kimberly had been reading a book where she sat on the bed. She heard a key in her hotel room door. She looked up, expecting to see Longarm sweep into the room and tell her about some fantastic place he would take her to dinner. She'd heard about the sumptuous selection of foods in San Francisco.

Two men burst into the room, and one grabbed her before she could scream. His hand came over her mouth, and his other arm tightened around her neck. They were Chinese. One spoke softly to her in perfect English.

"If you value your life, Miss Walkenhorst, you will not scream, or cause any disturbance. You will come with us quietly and you will understand that the life of your friend, Longarm, depends on how well you cooperate."

She tried to bite the man's hand. He hit her in the side and she tasted bile in her mouth. For a moment she thought she would pass out, but she didn't.

"Will you cooperate, Miss Walkenhorst, or should we tie and gag you and take you out in a laundry cart?"

The fingers eased on her mouth.

"I'll cooperate," she said quietly but loud enough so the man could hear. He was Chinese, she knew, but wore Western clothes, on the flashy side, and he had no Chinese pigtail down his back. His short, dark hair was cut in the current style.

The hand came away from her mouth cautiously.

"I said I'll cooperate with you. But you better not have hurt Longarm, or I'll kill both of you."

The taller of the Chinese laughed with little humor. "That I doubt, Kimberly, but I'd be disappointed if you didn't try. Loyalty is extremely important. Now, a sweater or coat for you and we'll be on our way."

They left by the rear door into the alley. They walked out to the street and down a block, then into another alley, and by that time Kimberly was totally lost. They came at last to another alley and went through an unmarked door. There were several dimly lighted passageways, and then they climbed stairs to the top of a four-story building. It had hissing gaslights and seemed to be some sort of a club.

At least fifty Chinese men sat in the room. It had a high ceiling and intense lights near the center, where a small platform rose above the chairs.

"We'll come back here later," the tall Chinese man said and led her to a door. Behind it she found a large bathroom, with a steel tub at one end and buckets of steaming water. On a low table sat a young Chinese girl who evidently had just bathed. Two Chinese women rubbed her dry with large white towels. A stunning gold decorated dress lay on the platform, and soon the women dressed the girl in the beautiful dress and piled her luxuriant black hair high on top of her head.

The girl turned, and Kimberly saw that she was young—fifteen, sixteen. She seemed to be in a daze. She moved when the women talked to her. Kimberly stood too far away to see her eyes.

The man holding Kimberly's arm walked her forward toward the tub.

"I'll leave you here, Miss Walkenhorst. Soon you'll take a bath and then be dressed for a special occasion. Don't worry, we haven't harmed Longarm. He's free and running around San Francisco. I'll be back shortly."

Two Chinese women caught her elbows and led her to the tub. They stripped her and motioned for her to get into the hot water. It had been laced with some sweet-smelling liquids and bubble soap.

The two women scrubbed her, but did not wash her dark brown hair. Instead they piled it high on her head.

They gave her something to drink, and she gulped it down quickly, then tried to taste it.

Soon the bath was over, and the women dried her, then dressed her in a dazzling gown decorated with lavish silver designs. The dress was heavy with the real silver. Slowly Kimberley realized she couldn't see as well as she normally could. She felt listless and sleepy. They had drugged her with something, and now she knew she couldn't do a thing about it. The other girl, who had had the bath before her, had had her lips painted and her cheeks powdered and given a touch of rouge. The same tall Chinese man who spoke English led Kimberly out of the bathroom into the larger area, where the fifty men had sat smoking.

155

Kimberly knew she had to get away. She tried to walk to another door she saw on the far side of the room, but one of the Chinese women shouted at her, caught her easily, and led her back to the dressing area.

She had her face painted and powdered and her hair pinned up higher and combed and brushed. Then they led her toward the door she had come in and waited.

The tall Chinese man came in and bowed and nodded when he looked at her. He said something in what she decided must be Chinese, and the women bowed and backed away.

"Now, Kimberly, it's time for the festivities. We've never used more than two girls in an evening, and we don't expect to do so tonight, but you are our reserve just in case we need you. You are strikingly beautiful tonight, Miss Walkenhorst, in that silver gown."

"I want to get out of here," she said. Kimberly was surprised at the sound of her own voice. It was slow, lower-pitched than usual, and didn't sound like her. She thought she could run out the door. Yes, she'd just run away from them all. She took the first step toward the door. She stumbled and almost fell. Her feet felt like lead. She couldn't run. She had trouble even walking.

Kimberly shut her eyes. Everything turned fuzzy. She blinked, but the whole place looked fuzzy and now pink, then blue. For a moment, it became all red and green; then it faded back to nearly normal. Normal but blurred around the edges. Now she was sure they had drugged her.

"Time to go, little sweetheart," the tall Chinese said. He led her, moving slowly to her pace. They went through the big door and into the hall, where all the men sat in circles around the stage. They had cards or tiles. They were betting at a furious, wild pace, shouting and calling back and forth.

Kimberly stopped when she saw the girl seated in a beautiful throne-like chair on the platform in the middle of the Chinese men.

The men in the chairs were all Chinese, both young and old. Most of them had the long black pigtails down their backs.

The girl in the chair held something. Kimberly couldn't see what it was.

"It's a little game we play," the tall Chinese man said to Kimberly. "You may have heard that we Chinese like to gamble. We'll bet on anything. Remember the pretty girl you saw in the dressing room?"

Slowly Kimberly nodded.

"She's down there in the game right now. She isn't gambling; she's the performer. That's a revolver she's holding. Have you ever played roulette? That's the game with the wheel spinning around. We've started a new game we call six-gun roulette. There's just one bullet in a cylinder that will hold six. The game is to bet whether the round will be under the hammer when the princess down there pulls the trigger.

"Odds six to one, right? Interesting gamble. The girl gets paid, too. If the gun doesn't go off, she makes ten dollars. She has already played twice, and the gun hasn't fired."

Kimberly realized the Chinese man was talking slowly so she could understand him. She moved slow; she even thought slow. So the girl played the game; if she won, she got ten dollars. He didn't say what happened if she lost.

They walked to the back of the chairs, and Kimberly could see the girl on the throne chair clearly. A singsong Chinese voice shouted something. The men around the stage made last-minute bets; then the voice barked another order and the betting stopped.

Everyone looked at the girl. She held out the revolver and pushed a device through the six chambers to prove that all were empty. Then she handed the revolver to a short, fat Chinese man, who held up one round that looked as if it had been painted silver. He put the round in one of the chambers and removed his hand so they could see that he had loaded just one round.

He snapped the cylinder back in place and handed it to the girl.

Now Kimberly could see that the girl was lethargic. She looked at the fat man who had given her the gun. She held it a moment.

The fat man barked two Chinese words at her. She lifted the six-gun and spun the cylinder. Then she spun it again and again. When she had twirled the device holding the round six times, she stopped.

The fat man stood ten feet from her, and now he shouted a number of Chinese words at her.

Her hand shook as she lifted the small-caliber revolver and pointed it at the side of her head just over her ear.

"Oh, no!" Kimberly shouted, but her words came out slow and soft. Even as they died among the murmurs and calls from the audience, Kimberly could see the girl tighten her finger on the trigger.

The double-action hammer rose, then fell, and the shattering explosion of the revolver round in the room sounded like a hundred sticks of dynamite going off at once. Kimberly pushed both hands over her ears, but she couldn't close her eyes. She saw the terrible scene as the bullet jolted through the girl's head, slamming her out of the princess chair and showering one side of the circle's players with blood, brains, and bone shards.

There were shouts of winners and losers. No one paid any attention to the girl slumped half out of the princess chair. The tall Chinese man who spoke perfect English came up beside Kimberly.

"Damn, the odds are stacked against me tonight. That's the second one we've lost in just two hours." He took a deep breath and lifted his brows over almond-shaped eyes. "Well, Miss Kimberly Walkenhorst of Chicago. It looks like you get to play the part of the princess right now."

Chapter 17

United States Marshal Penrod Rudolph read the note Longarm handed him and shook his head.

"I'm sorry. San Francisco is a big place. You can't even be sure who took her. If she's in Chinatown, it'll be almost impossible to find her."

"It's got to be Chang Toy, so I have to find her," Longarm said, his lips tight. "That door with no handle is my only lead. I'm going in there now. You want my badge?"

Rudolph didn't hesitate. "No, we'll cover you officially somehow. You want two or three men with you?"

"I'll work better alone in there. But I do want a sawed-off shotgun. You have one?"

Ten minutes later, Longarm stood near the door with no handle. He had watched for five minutes and seen two older Chinese men pause at the door and knock before having it opened for them. He'd moved up closer and caught the series of knocks. It was two, then a pause, followed by three more.

He walked up in the darkness with the sawed-off weapon hard against his leg. He gave the knock signal and the door opened outward. He stepped inside with his Colt leading the way. The small Chinese man there in the semidarkness tried to run. Longarm clubbed him with the revolver, and he went down on the first step.

The marshal left him there, running up the steps two at a time. On the first level he paused. A door lead into the building. He opened it with caution. Inside he found only darkness and heard nothing. He closed it and raced up to the second, then the third floor.

Longarm stepped into a room where the stairs ended. A Chinese man came toward him with a short sword, hatred on his face. Longarm shot him in the shoulder, blasting him to the side and out of action.

The shot boomed like a thunderclap in the small room. A door opened across the way, and two more guards rushed out. Longarm lifted the shotgun and cocked the trigger. Both men wavered, then turned and darted back through the door they had just left.

Longarm chased them, kicked open the door, and waited. No gunfire broke the silence. He looked in the room, but saw only another hallway, with two doors opening off it. The two men had vanished. He ran to the first door. Locked. He moved on to the next one but discovered a small room with no one in it.

The marshal raced to the end of the hall, something driving him to hurry. He had to hurry. He didn't know why, but he felt that time was the most important element. He looked up and found another flight of steps. Taking them three at a time, Longarm quickly raced to the top and saw another a short hallway.

To the left stood a Chinese man with a ceremonial battle-ax four feet long and with a foot-wide blade. He took two steps forward before Longarm shot him in the thigh and he went down screaming in pain. Two more guards appeared at the door, and when Longarm swung up the sawed-off shotgun that hung by a cord around his neck, the guards backed away.

He followed them. They stopped at a door and knocked. A moment later a man came out. In the dim glow of the gaslights, Longarm made out the frowning face of Chang Toy.

"Toy, you bastard. You kidnapped Kimberly. Where is she?"

Toy laughed.

From ten feet away, Longarm shot him in the right shoulder with the Colt .44–40. The gunshot boomed in the room, almost covering Toy's screams of pain. He slammed backward against the door, jarring it open. Longarm rushed forward, pushing him on inside and covering the room with the shotgun.

Two persons lounged in a luxurious living room. In it were some overstuffed chairs, a couch, and a low table with fruit and drinks on it. Longarm looked closer at the occupants.

"About time you rescued us, Longarm," Riane Moseley said. "This slant-eye has been holding us prisoner."

"Not a chance. I saw you go with his people willingly."

"We thought then that he would buy the diamonds. I told him you took my half. Eric won't even tell me where he hid his half."

Toy got to his feet from where he had fallen. His left hand held his blood-smeared right shoulder.

"I must get to a doctor," he said. He headed for a door. Longarm tripped him, sprawling him on the carpeted floor.

"For that you will die, Longarm," Toy hissed from the floor. Longarm shrugged and put his boot on the Chinaman's throat.

"You tell me where Kimberly is or you'll die in about twenty seconds."

"I don't know any Kimberly."

Longarm pushed down with his boot, with not quite enough force to crush Toy's windpipe but enough to cut off his air supply. The deputy U.S. marshal held his boot there for ten seconds and then let up.

Toy lay there gagging and holding his throat. Longarm searched the Chinese and took a derringer from him, then pulled him to his feet.

"Now," Longarm said. "Right now you take me to Kimberly or you'll die by inches. First I'll blow your elbows apart. Then if we don't get to Kimberly, I'll do the same thing to your knees, and you'll never walk another step in your life."

Toy stared at him and sneered. "I don't know where she is. It's a big building."

Longarm slashed the side of his six-gun into the bloody bullet hole on Toy's shoulder. The smartly dressed Chinese roared in pain and fury. When he had controlled his rage, he bit his lip until blood came. Then as the pain subsided, he motioned. "Through that door, down four doors. Perhaps we can find where she is."

"You better be telling me the truth, Chinaman, or you're as dead as Deputy Jones. You had him killed in that restaurant today. I don't know how, but you did. Now move!"

Riane and Eric stood. "You want us to come with you?"

"Yes. You heard anything about another white girl in here?"

"Yes. I saw her. They were getting her ready for something called princess roulette."

Longarm jabbed Toy with the Colt. "What's this princess roulette?"

"Just a game that the old men play. They're too jaded for sex or the pipe. They want something stimulating, exciting."

"Let's go see it, Toy. Any mistakes and you're a cripple—for life."

A half hour before Longarm had arrived in the Chinese building, Kimberly Walkenhorst looked at the tall Chinese man who spoke perfect English, and she tried to frown. She was having trouble concentrating. Her mind seemed like mush. For a moment she forgot where she was.

"What princess?" she asked. At once she wasn't sure why she had asked it. She looked at the man again.

"Come this way, Kimberly."

She frowned for a moment, then moved with him, her steps slow, a little awkward. She wasn't sure what she did or why. But the man had commanded her. She did as he said.

They walked to the edge of the platform. The old Chinese men chattered and laughed and waved money and markers at one another in a frenzy of betting.

The tall Chinese man took Kimberly's face in both his hands. "Your name is Kim. I am giving you to Mr. Soong, who will tell you what to do. Have you ever fired a revolver?"

Slowly she nodded.

"Good. You will do exactly what Mr. Soong tells you to do. Do you understand?"

"Yes." The word was slurred. She stared at the Chinese man's eyes. They were deep and black and endless. For a moment, panic shook her as she feared she might fall into the abyss.

Soong stepped up and put out his hands to hold her face, make her look at him. His eyes were just as deep and bottomless as the other man's. He spoke with a softer tone, more pleasant, kinder.

162

"Kim, you are our princess," he said in English. "You will do exactly as I tell you. Now come to the princess chair. It is ready for you. Your subjects are waiting."

He led her up two steps to the gold-and-silver-decorated chair with a high back and golden arm rests. She sat down and the old Chinese men cheered.

Soong brought something to her. It was heavy. He placed it on her lap and put her hands on it.

"This is your magic wand," he told her. She looked at it, but everything turned all fuzzy again and her head hurt.

"Magic wand," she said, slurring the words.

"Yes, and you must wave it when I tell you to. Do you understand?"

"Yes. Understand." Not even the slurred words or her tone of voice surprised her. Now she wanted only to do what her master, the king, commanded her. She looked into Soong's eyes again and fell into the bottomless chasm. For a moment she feared she would never come out of it.

Soong put her hand on the silver revolver. He put her finger on the trigger.

"This is the magic wand. You must move it when I tell you to. Do you understand? Don't pull the trigger until I tell you."

Kimberly felt a wave of nausea sweep over her. She fought against it, then blinked and tried to cut through the fuzzy haze, but nothing came clear.

"Kimberly, do you understand? When I tell you to wave your magic wand, you will bring it to your head and pull on the trigger. Do you understand?"

She didn't reply.

He moved her finger from the trigger and lifted the six-gun to her temple.

"When I tell you to wave your wand, you will lift it this way, put the end against your head, and pull on the trigger with your finger. Do you understand?"

"Yes, lift the wand and pull on the trigger. Understand."

"Good, good." The Chinese man turned and shouted something in Mandarin. The flurry of betting quieted, then stopped altogether.

163

Two old men in the front row shouted at Soong in Chinese. He listened, then shrugged. He chanted something, and the betting began again.

Soong turned to Kim. "You have a short time to wait, but remember what you are supposed to do. When I tell you to wave the wand, what do you do, Kim?"

She stared at him. It was so fuzzy, so . . . so confusing.

"What are you supposed to do, Kimberly?" Soong caught her face in his hands, and his black, evil eyes were only inches from hers. She stared at them and fell into the darkness of the void, and there was nothing to do, even to consider, except to do exactly as he said.

"I . . . I will raise the wand to my head and then pull the trigger."

"Yes, yes. Good girl, Kim. Good girl."

On the fourth floor of the same building, Longarm prodded Chang Toy down the hallway.

"How far is it? Where are we going?"

"To the game room," Toy said. Blood seeped from his shoulder, leaked between his fingers, and dripped on the varnished floor.

"How much farther?" Longarm asked, his lips a tight, hard line.

"Only a short way."

They went around a corner, and Longarm saw two guards ahead of them, both with holstered revolvers.

Chang Toy shouted something in Mandarin, and the guards dug for their weapons.

Longarm raised the shotgun and fired one round. The thirteen double-aught buck slugs of .32-caliber size knocked down both the guards. One never moved; the other tried to get out his six-gun. Longarm fired one shot from his Colt, and the man shuddered and lay still.

"Any more surprises and your elbow goes," Longarm snarled at Toy. "If we come to any more guards, you tell them to lay flat on the floor. You understand?"

Toy nodded.

"Where now?" Longarm asked. He had kept the two Chicago robbers moving with them. They seemed anxious to come along.

"Past those bodies," Toy said through gritted teeth. "Another door, then the game room."

"Kimberly better be there and safe and sound, or both your knees get blasted to hell. You hear me, Toy?"

Longarm saw the Chinese sweat, and he dubbed it a good sign. They passed the two dead guards and headed for the door across an empty room.

Just before they came to the door, Toy turned to Longarm.

"You must understand, I only work here. I work for Chop Soo as the rest of us do. Whatever happens is at his bidding. Whatever you find beyond the door is not my doing."

Longarm grabbed the back of his expensive suit coat and rammed him forward, pushing open the doors. Just inside the room, Longarm stopped him. He saw the big room, over a hundred feet across. In the center chairs were set around a small stage with sixty or seventy old Chinese men clustered in them. Then on the riser he saw a girl seated in a fancy throne chair.

He looked closer, then ran forward, ramming Chang Toy ahead of him.

When he was thirty feet away, he could see the girl in the chair plainly: Kimberly! She had just raised a silver six-gun and placed it against her temple.

"Nooooooooooooooooooooooooo!" Longarm bellowed and charged forward, knocking Toy to the floor as he raced toward the stage, his Colt out and ready. His only thought: Could he get there in time to save Kimberly?

Chapter 18

"Kimberly, no!" Longarm shouted again. He fired a round from his six-gun into the ceiling and charged past half a dozen surprised Chinese men with braids. Longarm watched Kimberly. She still had the weapon aimed at her head.

"No! Kimberly Walkenhorst, don't pull the trigger!"

Kimberly blinked and turned to look at the disturbance. Longarm ran into a Chinese guard who had risen from near the platform. Longarm's right fist smashed into the Oriental face, and it sagged and fell away. He charged onto the small stage, then stopped.

His voice was firm but friendly. "Kimberly, this is wrong. Don't do this. I'm Longarm, Kimberly, please put the gun down."

She looked at him, and slowly what he thought was recognition broke over her glazed features.

She frowned, stared to the side, at the weapon, and slowly took it away from her head. She glanced at Longarm a moment, then spotted Chang Toy at the edge of the platform, where Longarm had dumped him. Toy stood and took one look at Kimberly.

She swung the weapon around to aim it at Toy and pulled the trigger in one smooth move. The hammer fell on a live round and fired. Chang Toy gasped and grabbed his chest, then slowly slumped to his knees. Kimberly aimed again and pulled the trigger. The weapon fired again and then again and a fourth time. Four rounds plowed into Chang Toy's chest, his face registering surprise and then disbelief just before his eyes faded shut and he sprawled across the small platform.

Longarm dashed the ten feet to Kimberly and caught her hand. He took the gun from her and dropped it. He saw the glazed look still shrouding her eyes. She had been drugged. He picked her up and headed for the closest door. Two guards appeared in the opening, with six-guns. Longarm brought up the sawed-off shotgun with one hand and blasted a round at them. One fell; the other limped away. He reloaded the shotgun. He yelled at the two Chicago jewel robbers.

"Eric, Riane, the only way you'll get out of here alive is to come with us." The robbers didn't have to think it over. They turned and ran to Longarm. They all hurried out the door. In the hall stood four more guards, two with guns and two with long lances.

Longarm fired a round from the shotgun, scattering the guards, putting two of them on the floor. He quickly let Kimberly down and reloaded.

"I can walk now," Kimberly said. She grabbed at Riane to help her, and they all rushed down the hall to a stairway, thinking it must lead outside.

They dropped down the stairs to the third floor, found another hallway, and ran along that. Below them they saw a cluster of guards, all with guns drawn.

"Down this way," Longarm said. They ran along another hall, to stairs at the far end of the building. Only two guards there. Longarm fired with his Colt, wounding one man, driving the other one back.

That stairway led them to the second floor, and there they hunted a way to the first floor. Behind them they could hear a tide of footsteps running toward them.

"Let's go down that way!" Riane called. They found a window outside of which was a metal fire escape leading down twelve feet to the alley. Longarm sent Kimberly down first. She had come out of the drugging and was near normal. She took Longarm's derringer, holding the watch and weapon in one hand.

Riane went second and then Eric. Just as Eric levered through the window to the fire escape, six guards rushed into the hall.

Longarm drove them back with a round from the shotgun. He sent another load of double-aught buck down the hall, then reloaded the scattergun on his way down the steel ladders.

He was almost to the ground when gunfire erupted from above. He leaned out and fired once at the window with the shotgun, then hit the ground.

Kimberly had the two robbers under her derringer halfway to the street. Longarm caught up with them and raced ahead. They were still in Chinatown. They moved to the left. The street deadended.

Longarm headed the backtracking. Four Chinese men stared at them as they went by. Longarm raised the sawed-off shotgun, and the men vanished down an alley.

It took them fifteen minutes to find their way out of Chinatown. Then Longarm hailed a cab, and in another ten minutes they arrived at the Federal Building. The front door was locked.

Longarm pounded on the door for two minutes before a janitor came and opened it.

"I'm a federal marshal," Longarm said. "Is Marshal Rudolph still in his office?"

The maintenance man shrugged.

Longarm led his parade up the stairs to the second floor office and smiled when he saw light coming under the marshal's door. He pushed inside.

A half hour later, Longarm had told the marshal about the confrontation and that there were bound to be four or five dead Chinese men in that building.

"That won't give us any trouble," Marshal Rudolph said. "San Francisco police will never know about those dead men. Chop Soo takes care of his own down there. The dead will be buried, and the living Chinese will be punished."

He looked at Kimberly. "Those men were gambling whether or not the live round would come up ready to fire when the trigger was pulled! I find it hard to understand how human beings . . ." He stopped. "Sometimes the Chinese have strange customs and amusements. I hardly think . . ."

Longarm shook his head. "It wasn't much of a gamble that last time. They must have fixed the weapon so it had five rounds already in it, then ceremoniously added the sixth. Or maybe they switched it for a loaded gun. No gamble at all. The men who knew the gun would fire on any cylinder must have cleaned up at thirty-to-one odds."

"The drug they gave you, child, any idea what it was?" Marshal Rudolph asked.

"I don't have the faintest idea. After ten minutes it made me do anything that Mr. Soong told me to do. Then Longarm told me *not* to do something, and I followed his orders. When that happened, I came out of it a little. I remember seeing Chang Toy, and I turned."

Her eyes went wide. "Did I shoot at . . . ?" She shook her head. "No that's impossible. I couldn't do that. I have fired a revolver lots of times. My father taught me to shoot one summer. But I could never . . ."

Longarm broke in. "I don't know what you're imagining. Right after I yelled at you to move the gun, you pulled it down and dropped it. Well, looks like this little phase of our operation is almost over. All we need now is the other half of the Chicago jewels. I'd think Eric must be glad enough to be alive, after his rescue from Chinatown, to tell us where he hid them."

"Bad guess, Longarm," Eric said. "I'd have made it out of there somehow. Of course, I'd already figured that Riane would be the next roulette princess."

Riane turned to him, eyes wide. "You would have sold me to them for your freedom. I knew it. I knew I should never trust an actor. My father told me that three years ago. If I knew where you hid those stones, I'd tell Longarm myself."

"You have nothing to lose anymore after your stupid trick back in Colorado," Eric said. "I have fifty thousand dollars to lose."

"And lose it you will, Heinrich," Longarm said. "Just you and me in a small room and in fifteen minutes, either you tell me where the gems are or you'll never walk again. How would you like that, badman?"

Eric scowled and looked at Marshal Rudolph. "You hear that! He threatened to torture me! That's against the law. I want to file a complaint against this deputy right now."

Marshal Rudolph stared at him. "What was that? I'm getting a little hard of hearing."

Eric's scowl turned into disbelief.

"Damn, getting so you can't trust anybody anymore."

Kimberly had been listening. She eyed Eric curiously.

"Eric, I don't see how you can stand to wear that heavy coat. It's so warm in here I'm about ready to pass out."

"I'm fine. I get cold easily."

"I bet you do," Kimberly said. "Let's see how cold you get. Longarm, help me take Eric's coat off. It has a thick, lumpy lining in it. Look, Eric is really starting to sweat now."

"No, I'm just fine."

"Eric, for an actor, that's a terrible reading of the line," Longarm said. "Get a little heart into it, make us believe you."

"All right, I'll take it off, not important. What I want to know is how you can charge me with jewel robbery when you don't have any gems. You found Riane with some, but not me. So, if there's no charges, I'll be leaving."

"Not a chance," Longarm said. "Give me the coat."

Ten minutes later they had ripped the lining half out of the coat and found a handful of diamonds and a few rubies and emeralds. They would get the rest of them where they had been sewn into the lining.

"How did you know?" Longarm asked Kimberly.

"Riane said he always carried the gems with him, but today he didn't have a bag or big pockets or a money belt. He had no place to hide the jewels. I figured they had to be in the coat. That one is far too heavy for the mild San Francisco climate."

The robbers were both booked in the San Francisco jail and put on hold for Chicago authorities. The jewels went into a box, were counted, cataloged, evaluated, and kept in the safe in the marshal's office until the Chicago representative appeared.

Longarm and Marshal Rudolph grinned at each other.

"I'm not sure about that China connection with the robbers," Longarm said. "But it certainly did provide a roadmap for us to use to find the Chicago robbers in Chinatown."

"We're sure Chop Soo is bringing in a lot of merchandise, the expensive kind that doesn't get charged duty," Marshal Rudolph said. "We'll be watching him again. Without his right-hand man Chang Toy, he'll have a harder time dealing with us round-eyes."

Kimberly made a face. "I've still got a bad taste in my mouth from that drug. I wonder what it was. I think a late-night snack might be good. Are there any restaurants still open?"

They found one open and serving.

Later that night in their room at the hotel, Kimberly showed Longarm just how much she appreciated his help.

"If you hadn't charged in right then, I'd have blown a hole right through my head," Kimberly said. "That drug made me the slave of whoever talked to me. It was frightening, weird, crazy. I don't want ever to experience anything like that again."

"I hope you won't have to."

"Longarm?"

He turned in the bed and looked at her. The light made the red glints in her long brown hair more pronounced where it fell and half-covered one breast. "Yes?"

"What happens now?"

"Tomorrow we go to the telegraph office and send wires to our bosses. You tell yours that the balance of the gems have been found. Probably at least 95 percent of them have been recovered. Your pay and bonus is due on the whole entire one hundred thousand dollars.

"I'll send a wire to my boss, Billy Vail in Denver, telling him that I have two more days of work here to clean up the final bits and pieces of this case, then I'll be heading back to Denver."

"So in the next two days we should be able to go swimming in the Pacific Ocean?" she asked.

Longarm laughed. This girl would get him into trouble yet. "You are crazy. The water is probably fifty-two degrees out there. You'll freeze both of your . . . your nose off."

"So I'll freeze a little. You'll be there to thaw me out and get me real warm again."

Longarm watched her. If she wanted to go swimming in ice water, he'd see that she did. But that didn't mean he had to be crazy. Thinking about it again, he decided that somehow he'd get tricked into swimming, so he might as well be ready for it.

Billy Vail wasn't going to believe this. But then it would be a week or so before he'd have to face Billy, looking for a new assignment.

A sleek, sexy, and naked body rolled on top of Longarm's lean form.

"Once more, Longarm. Let's see if we can get really inventive this time."

They did.

Watch for

LONGARM AND THE BORDER SHOWDOWN

174th in the bold LONGARM series from Jove

Coming in June!

Omaha, Nebraska, Early Spring, 1866

Construction Engineer Glenn Gilchrist stood on the melting surface of the frozen Missouri River with his heart hammering his rib cage. Poised before him on the eastern bank of the river was the last Union Pacific supply train asked to make this dangerous river crossing before the ice broke to flood south. The temperatures had soared as an early chinook had swept across the northern plains and now the river's ice was sweating like a fat man in July. A lake of melted ice was growing deeper by the hour and there was still this last critical supply train to bring across.

"This is madness!" Glenn whispered even as the waiting locomotive puffed and banged with impatience while huge crowds from Omaha and Council Bluffs stomped their slushy shorelines to keep their feet warm. Fresh out of the Harvard School of Engineering. Glenn had measured and remeasured the depth and stress-carrying load of the rapidly melting river yet still could not be certain if it would support the tremendous weight of this last supply train. But Union Pacific's vice president, Thomas Durant, had given the bold order that it was to cross, and there were enough fools to be found willing to man the train and its supply cars, so here Glenn was, standing in the middle of the Missouri and about half sure he was about to enter a watery grave.

177

Suddenly, the locomotive engineer blasted his steam whistle and leaned out his window. "We got a full head of steam and the temperature is risin', Mr. Gilchrist!"

Glenn did not hear the man because he was imagining what would happen the moment the ice broke through. Good Lord, they could all plunge to the bottom of Big Muddy and be swept along under the ice for hundreds of miles to a frozen death. A vision flashed before Glenn's eyes of an immense ragged hole in the ice fed by two sets of rails feeding into the cold darkness of the Missouri River.

The steam whistle blasted again. Glenn took a deep breath, raised his hand, and then chopped it down an if he were swinging an ax. Cheers erupted from both riverbanks and the locomotive jerked tons of rails, wooden ties, and track-laying hardware into motion.

Glenn swore he could feel the weakening ice heave and buckle the exact instant the Manchester locomotive's thirty tons crunched its terrible weight onto the river's surface. Glenn drew in a sharp breath. His eyes squinted into the blinding glare of ice and water as the railroad tracks swam toward the advancing locomotive through melting water. The sun bathed the rippling surface of the Missouri River in a shimmering brilliance. The engineer began to blast his steam whistle and the crowds roared at each other across the frozen expanse. Glenn finally expelled a deep breath, then started to backpedal as he motioned the locomotive forward into railroading history.

Engineer Bill Donovan was grinning like a fool and kept yanking on the whistle cord, egging on the cheering crowds.

"Slow down!" Glenn shouted at the engineer, barely able to hear his own voice as the steam whistle continued its infernal shriek.

But Donovan wasn't about to slow down. His unholy grin was as hard as the screeching iron horse he rode and Glenn could hear Donovan shouting to his firemen to shovel faster. Donovan was pushing him, driving the locomotive ahead as if he were intent on forcing Glenn aside and charging across the river to the other side.

"Slow down!" Glenn shouted, backpedaling furiously.

But Donovan wouldn't pull back on his throttle, which left

Glenn with just two poor choices. He could either leap aside and let the supply train rush past, or he could try to swing on board and wrestle its control from Donovan. It might be the only thing that would keep the ice from swallowing them alive.

Glenn chose the latter. He stepped from between the shivering rails, and when Donovan and his damned locomotive charged past drenching him in a bone-chilling shoot of lee water, Glenn lunged for the platform railing between the cab and the coal tender. The locomotive's momentum catapulted him upward to sprawl between the locomotive and tender.

"Dammit!" he shouted, clambering to his feet. "The ice isn't thick enough to take both the weight and a pounding! You were supposed to . . ."

Glenn's words died in his throat an instant later when the ice cracked like rifle fire and thin, ragged schisms fanned out from both sides of the tracks. At the same time, the rails and the ties they rested upon rolled as if supported by the storm-tossed North Atlantic.

"Jesus Christ!" Donovan shouted, his face draining of color and leaving him ashen. "We're going under!"

"Throttle down!" Glenn yelled an he jumped for the brake.

The locomotive's sudden deceleration threw them both hard against the firebox, searing flesh. The fireman's shovel clattered on the dock an his face corroded with terror and the ice splintered outward from them with dark tentacles.

"Steady!" Glenn ordered, grabbing the young man's arm because he was sure the kid was about to jump from the coal tender. "Steady now!"

The next few minutes were an eternity but the ice held as they crossed the center of the Missouri and rolled slowly toward the Nebraska shore.

"Come on!" a man shouted from Omaha. "Come on!"

Other watchers echoed the cry an the spectators began to take heart.

"We're going to make it, sir!" Donovan breathed, banging Glenn on the shoulder. "Mr. Gilchrist, we're by Gawd goin' to make it!"

"Maybe. But if the ice breaks behind us, the supply cars will drag us into the river. If that happens, we jump and take our chances."

"Yes, sir!" the big Irishman shouted, his square jaw bumping rapidly up and down.

Donovan reeked of whiskey and his eyes were bright and glassy. Glenn turned to look at the young fireman. "Mr. Chandlis, have you been drinking too?"

"Not a drop, sir." Young Sean Chandlis pointed to shore and cried, "Look, Mr. Gilchrist, we've made it!"

Glenn felt the locomotive bump onto the tracks resting on the solid Nebraska riverbank. Engineer Donovan blasted his steam whistle and nudged the locomotive's throttle causing the big drivers to spin a little as they surged up the riverbank. Those same sixty-inch driving wheels propelled the supply cars into Omaha where they were enfolded by the jubilant crowd.

The scene was one of pandemonia as Donovan kept yanking on his steam whistle and inciting the crowd. Photographers crowded around the locomotive taking pictures.

"Come on and smile!" Donovan shouted in Glenn's ear. "We're heroes!"

Glenn didn't feel like smiling. His knees wanted to buckle from the sheer relief of having this craziness behind his. He wanted to smash Donovan's grinning face for starting across the river too fast and for drinking on duty. But the photographers kept taking pictures and all that Glenn did was to bat Donovan's hand away from the infernal steam whistle before it drove him mad.

God, the warm, fresh chinook winds felt fine on his cheeks and it was good to be still alive. Glenn waved to the crowd and his eyes lifted back to the river that he know would soon be breaking up if this warm weather held. He turned back to gaze westward and up to the city of Omaha. Omaha—when he'd arrived last fall, it had still been little more than a tiny riverfront settlement. Today, it could boast a population of more than six thousand, all anxiously waiting to follow the Union Pacific rails west.

"We did it!" Donovan shouted at the crowd as he rained his fists in victory. "We did it!"

Glenn saw a tall beauty with reddish hair pushing forward through the crowd, struggling mightily to reach the supply train. "Who is that?"

Donovan followed his eyes. "Why, that's Mrs. Megan Gallagher. Ain't she and her sister somethin', though!"

Glenn had not even noticed the smaller woman with two freckled children in tow who was also waving to the train and trying to follow her sister to its side. Glenn's brow furrowed. "Are their husbands on this supply train?"

Donovan's wide grin dissolved. "Well, Mr. Gilchrist, I know you told everyone that only single men could take this last one across, but . . ."

Glenn clenched his fists in surprise and anger. "Donovan, don't you understand that the Union Pacific made it clear that there was to be no drinking and no married men on this last run! Dammit, you broke both rules! I've got no choice but to fire all three of you."

"But, sir!"

Glenn felt sick at heart but also betrayed. Bill "Wild Man" Donovan was probably the best engineer on the payroll but he'd proved he was also an irresponsible fool, one who played to the crowd and was more than willing to take chances with other men's lives and the Union Pacific's rolling stock and precious construction supplies.

"I'm sorry, Donovan. Collect your pay from the paymaster before quitting time," Glenn said, swinging down from the cab into the pressing crowd. Standing six feet three inches, Glenn was tall enough to look over the sea of humanity and note that Megan Gallagher and her sister were embracing their triumphant husbands. It made Glenn feel even worse to think that those two men would be without jobs before this day was ended.

Men pounded Glenn an the back in congratulations but he paid them no mind as he pushed through the crowd, moving off toward the levee where these last few vital tons of rails, ties, and other hardware were being stored until the real work of building a railroad finally started.

"Hey!" Donovan shouted, overtaking Glenn and pulling him up short. "You can't fire me! I'm the best damned engineer you've got!"

"Were the best," Glenn said, tearing his arm free, "now step aside."

But Donovan didn't budge. The crowd pushed around the two large men, clearly puzzled as to the matter of this dispute in the wake of such a bold and daring success only moments earlier.

"What'd he do wrong?" a man dressed in a tailored suit asked in a belligerent voice. "By God, Bill Donovan brought that train across the river and that makes him a hero in my book!"

This assessment was loudly applauded by others. Glenn could feel resentment building against him as the news of his decision to fire three of the crew swept through the crowd. "This is a company matter. I don't make the rules, I just make sure that they are followed."

Donovan chose to appeal to the crowd. "Now you hear that, folks. Mr. Gilchrist is going to fire three good men without so much as a word of thanks. And that's what the working man gets from this railroad for risking his life!"

"Drop it." Glenn told the big Irishman. "There's nothing left to be gained from this."

"Isn't there?"

"No."

"You're making a mistake." Donovan said, playing to the crowd. The confident Irishman thrust his hand out with a grin. "So why don't we let bygones be bygones and go have a couple of drinks to celebrate? Gallagher and Fox are two of the best men on the payroll. They deserve a second chance. Think about the fact they got wives and children."

Glenn shifted uneasily. "I'll talk to Fox and Gallagher but you were in charge and I hold you responsible."

"Hell, we made it in grand style, didn't we!"

"Barely," Glenn said, "and you needlessly jeopardized the crew and the company's assets, that's why you're still fired." Donovan flushed with anger. "You're a hard, unforgiving man, Gilchrist."

"And you are a fool when you drink whiskey. Later, I'll hear Fox's and Gallagher's excuses."

"They drew lots for a cash bonus ride across that damned melting river!" Donovan swore, his voice hardening. "Gallagher and Fox needed the money!"

"The Union Pacific didn't offer any bonus! It was your job to ask for volunteers and choose the best to stop forward."

Donovan shrugged. He had a lantern jaw, and heavy, fist-scarred brows overhanging a pair of now very angry and bloodshot eyes. "The boys each pitched in a couple dollars into a pot. I'll admit it was my idea. But the winners stood to earn fifty dollars each when we crossed."

"To leave wives and children without support?" Glenn snapped. "That's a damned slim legacy."

"These are damned slim times." Donovan said. "The idea was, if we drowned, the money would be used for the biggest funeral and wake Omaha will ever see. And if we made it . . . well, you saw the crowd."

"Yeah," Glenn said. "If you won, you'd flood the saloons and drink it up so either way all the money would go for whiskey."

"Some to the wives and children," Donovan said quietly.

"Like hell."

Glenn started to turn and leave the man but Donovan's voice stopped him cold. "If you turn away, I'll drop you," the Irishman warned in a soft, all the more threatening voice.

"That would be a real mistake," Glenn said.

Although several inches taller than the engineer, Glenn had no illusions as to matching the Irishman's strength or fighting ability. Donovan was built like a tree stump and was reputed to be one of the most vicious brawlers in Omaha. If Glenn had any advantage, it was that he had been on Harvard's collegiate boxing club and gained some recognition for quickness and a devastating left hook that had surprised and then floored many an opponent.

"Come on, sir," Donovan said with a friendly wink as he reached into his coat pocket and dragged out a pint of whiskey. The engineer uncorked and extended it toward Glenn. "So I got a little carried away out there. No harm, was there?"

"I'm sorry," Glenn said, pivoting around on his heel and starting off toward the levee to oversee the stockpiling and handling of this last vital shipment.

This time when Donovan's powerful fingers dug into Glenn's shoulder to spin him around, Glenn dropped into a slight crouch, whirled, and drove his left hook upward with every ounce of power he could muster. The punch caught Donovan in the gut. The big Irishman's cheeks blew out and his eyes bugged. Glenn pounded him again in the solar plexus and Donovan staggered, his face turning fish-belly white. Glenn rocked back and threw a textbook combination of punches to the bigger man's face that split Donovan's cheek to the bone and dropped him to his knees.

"You'd better finish me!" Donovan gasped. " 'Cause I swear to settle this score!"

Glenn did not take the man's threat lightly. He cocked back his fist but he couldn't deliver the knockout blow, not while the engineer was gasping in agony. "Stay away from me," Glenn warned before he hurried away.

He felt physically and emotionally drained by the perilous river crossing and his fight with Donovan. He had been extremely fortunate to survive both confrontations. It had reinforced the idea in his mind that he was not seasoned enough to be making such critical decisions. It wasn't that he didn't welcome responsibility, for he did. But not so much and not so soon.

The trouble was that the fledgling Union Pacific itself was in over its head. No one know from one day to the next whether it would still be in operation or who was actually in charge. From inception, Vice President Thomas Durant, a medical doctor turned railroad entrepreneur, was the driving force behind getting the United States Congress to pass two Pacific Railway Acts through Congress. With the Civil War just ending and the nation still numb from the shock of losing President Abraham Lincoln, the long discussed hope of constructing a transcontinental railroad was facing tough sledding. Durant himself was sort of an enigma, a schemer and dreamer whom some claimed was a charlatan while others thought he possessed a brilliant organizational mind.

Glenn didn't know what to think of Durant. It had been through him that he'd landed this job fresh out of engineering school as his reward for being his class valedictorian. So far, Glenn's Omaha experience had been nothing short of chaotic. Lacking sufficient funds and with the mercurial Durant dashing back and forth to Washington, there had been a clear lack of order and leadership. It had been almost three years since Congress had agreed to pay both the Union Pacific and the Central Pacific Railroads the sums of $16,000 per mile for track laid over the plains, $32,000 a mile through the arid wastes of the Great Basin, and a whopping $48,000 per mile for track laid over the Rocky and the Sierra Nevada mountain ranges.

Now, with the approach of spring, the stage had been set to finally begin the transcontinental race. One hundred miles of roadbed had been graded westward from Omaha and almost forty miles of temporary track had been laid. For two years, big paddlewheel steamboats had been carrying mountains of supplies up the Missouri River. There were three entire locomotives still packed in shipping crates resting on the levee while two more stood assembled beside the Union Pacific's massive new brick roundhouse with its ten locomotive repair pits. Dozens of hastily constructed shops and offices surrounded the new freight and switching yards.

There was still more work than men and that was a blessing for veterans in the aftermath of the Civil War joblessness and destruction. Every day, dozens more ex-soldiers and fortune seekers crossed the Missouri River into Omaha and signed on with the Union Pacific Railroad. Half a nation away, the Central Pacific Railroad was already attacking the Sierra Nevada Mountains but Glenn had heard that they were not so fortunate in hiring men because of the stiff competition from the rich gold and silver mines on the Comstock Lode.

Glenn decided he would have a few drinks along with some of the other officers of the railroad, then retire early. He was dog-tired and the strain of these last few days of worrying about the stress-carrying capacity of the melting ice had enervated him to the point of bone weariness.

Glenn realized he would be more than glad when the generals finally arrived to take command of the Union Pacific. He would be even happier when the race west finally began in dead earnest.